ANGELINA
THE
LOST PRINCESS

ALEXA BOOKER

ASH Brothers Group, LLC, *Publishers*
Copyright © 2021 Alexa Booker All rights reserved

First edition, 2021 / Layout Design by Antoine Holmes

Art Direction by: Antoine Holmes
ISBN: 978-0-578-89014-2

Dedication Quote

To Daddy -
who helped kickstart this story

&

To Mama
who worked hard to support me

PROLOGUE

FOR MANY YEARS, there was a beautiful world called Magictopia. It was a magical land where mystical beings lived. It was ruled by a kind and noble queen who prospered the land. But the peace was broken by the queen's envious twin sister, who attacked in the hopes of taking the kingdom for her own. The queen defeated her sister, and the peace ruled again. Years later, the queen's sister came back, taking over the kingdom and killing the queen and the king. But before her death, the queen sent her daughter to Earth through a magic portal for safety. Fourteen years later…

CHAPTER ONE
ANGELINA

"GIRLS, BREAKFAST!" shouted Ms. A, cooking scrambled eggs.

"Coming!" said Angelina, putting on her blue baseball cap from her favorite team and heading for the stairs.

Angelina was fourteen years old; she had rich chocolate skin with voluminous black curls reaching her shoulders and dark brown eyes that were like lavish deep pools of honey. She was a tall, slim girl who wore a long-sleeved white shirt with green stripes and jean shorts with sneakers. She also wore a beautiful golden heart locket that she had since she was a baby.

Angelina had long dreamed of going to Rainbow Waters, but she had to wait until she got into high school. Rainbow Waters was the best high school in New York. Everyone there was kind and respectful, and they had all sorts of different clubs, after-school activities, and much more. Now she was a freshman and could go to the high school of her dreams. She slid down the staircase and sat down at the table.

"You're early as usual," said Ms. A, handing Angelina a plate of scrambled eggs.

"Of course, it's my first day at Rainbow Waters, and I've been waiting forever to go there," said Angelina with an excited smile on her face.

Ms. A was a kind woman. Her skin was olive-brown. She had short, straight, dark brown hair and trustful brown eyes that made Angelina feel safe and warm. She was a short and slim woman with a warm, matronly smile.

The other nine girls in the orphanage came down and took a seat at the table. They were between the ages of eight and seventeen. Leona, Sophia, and Avery groaned as they sat down.

"Why do we have to go to school?" groaned Leona.

"Each year adds more stress to my life!" whined Sophia.

"It's too much for my brain!" complained Avery.

Leona had dark skin with a spoon-shaped figure. She wore her hair in a big black afro with her huge brown eyes. Leona was fifteen years old and was always up for fun no matter what. She was a great party planner, which made her the wild card of the group. She could turn any bad day into a good one and always enjoyed making people happy.

Sophia was a thin girl with long, neat, straight blonde hair and brown eyes. Her passion was cheerleading.

She had been a cheerleader ever since she was five years old, and she dreamed of being a cheerleader at the NFL or NBA and cheer the teams on. She practiced every day, not only her cheers but also her flips and kicks, which made her the team captain of her cheer squad last year, and this year, she would be the same.

Avery was a petite girl with thin, black hair that she kept in a ponytail. Her eyes were gray with a hint of green. She was a quiet girl who liked reading, science, and doing all kinds of experiments. She won many awards from science fairs throughout the years, and she wanted to be a scientist and win the Nobel Peace Prize so she could make the world a better place. The girls were all fifteen, with the exception of Angelina, being fourteen.

"Oh, come on, girls," said Ms. A. "Angelina's going to the same school as you, and you don't hear her complaining."

"Yeah, guys, besides this time, we can all go together," said Angelina, trying to lift their spirits. She looked at her watch--it was 7:14. She grabbed her skateboard and headed outside.

"Bye, Ms.A!" She waved good-bye, and she skated off to school.

***

WHEN ANGELINA ARRIVED AT THE FRONT OF THE SCHOOL, she stared in amazement. The school was huge. It looked more like a college than a high school.

Angelina went inside, and it was even better than the front of the school. The walls were sky blue with golden letters that said.

"WELCOME STUDENTS TO ANOTHER YEAR AT RAINBOW WATERS!"

"Wow, it's just as great as I imagined!" Angelina said with a bright smile.

She began to spin gracefully with joy until she bumped into someone, making him trip and scatter his papers on the floor. The boy stood up and turned to Angelina. He had a tall, lean figure. His coily black hair was cut short, and his eyes were dark brown, as was his skin. He wore a white t-shirt with a jean jacket and jeans.

"I'm sorry, let me help you with those," Angelina offered. She stopped and helped him pick up his papers. "Sorry about that. I guess I didn't see where I was going," apologized Angelina.

"That's okay, that was a hit!" the boy joked.

"I'm Angelina." She put out her hand.

"I'm Max," said the boy, shaking her hand.

"I'm actually new here. I came from Richwood."

"Richwood? They are our biggest rival, and they're really competitive."

"That's Richwood for you." They laughed.

"Well, I better get going. Do you want a tour of the school?"

"No, thanks, I'm good," said Angelina.

"Alright, see ya around." Max waved good-bye and walked off. Angelina gestured back and smiled. She was glad she made a new friend.

She went on her way when a group of three girls stopped in front of her. The girl in the middle took a few steps closer towards Angelina. She had a slim hourglass figure and fair skin. Her long black hair was kept neat. She wore shimmering makeup, and her outfit was a purple glitter dress with a fur vest that she completed with heels and a purse. Her brown eyes stared at Angelina like a snake staring down a mouse.

"Um, can I help you?" asked Angelina.

"Well, you can start by knowing who I am," said the girl with an attitude.

"And who are you?" asked Angelina. The girl rolled her eyes.

"I'm Violet Crystal, my family owns one of the most successful companies in New York, and my clothes cost more than your life," Violet said, flipping her hair dramatically. "And since you're new here, I need to set some ground rules."

"You mean, the school rules?" Violet rolled her eyes.

"No, the rules I give around this school."

"Why?" asked Angelina, confused why some random person was bossing her around.

"Because my father owns one of the most successful companies in New York and the school's biggest sponsor. That means I'm in charge, and everyone obeys me."

It was true that Violet Crystal's family owned a hugely successful company, one of the biggest in New York. Her parents treated her like a princess, which caused her to be spoiled and vain. Violet acted like she was the queen, and the world was her kingdom. Everyone treated her like a queen and followed her orders, and if anyone did otherwise, they were disrespecting her. Or at least, it was what she thought.

"Why does being rich give you a good reason to tell me what to do?" asked Angelina, testing Violet's patience.

"Because if you don't, bad things will happen," said Violet with a bittersweet smile. "So I suggest that you know your place and stay there. Before someone has to do it for you." With that, she tossed her hair and walked off with the two girls following her. "Oh, and by the way," She stopped and turned back to Angelina. "Nice necklace. I almost believed you didn't get it from the dumpster." Violet and her entourage laughed as they walked away.

"Hey!" called Angelina. Violet turned around. "I don't know who you think you are, but you're not gonna boss me around like a slave. And you seriously need a reality check because that's not how you get respect." She turned her back, ready to walk away, but turned around to Violet.

"Oh, and by the way, you gotta tell me where you got that white rag from." She said with the same bittersweet smile Violet gave her. Knowing she had won that round, she walked off to class.

"She did not just say that!" said a furious Violet. "Who does that worthless lowlife think she is!?" She cooled herself and looked at Angelina. "We better keep an eye on her," she muttered. And she stormed off, stomping her heels as a loud warning to everyone in the halls.

CHAPTER TWO
AVERY

AS ANGELINA WALKED INTO MATH CLASS, she noticed Avery walking in as well.

"Hey, Avery!" she said.

"Oh, hey, it looks like we're going to be in the same class," said Avery, happy that they would be sharing.

They walked to their seats and sat down.

"Good morning, class! I'm Mr. Lean, and I'll be your teacher," said a middle-aged man. "Now, before we begin, we have a new student here." He looked at Angelina. "Why don't you tell us a little bit about yourself?" he said.

Angelina stood up.

"My name is Angelina Golden, and it has been my dream to go here, and I hope I have a good year here."

"Thank you, miss Golden," said Mr. Lean, giving her a nod to sit back down.

Angelina sat back in her seat.

"Now, does anyone have any questions?"

A young man raised his hand.

"Yes, Mr. Tube, do you have a question?" asked Mr. Lean.

"I've got a question: is it true that you lived the same time as the dinosaurs?" A boy blurted out, laughing.

Mr. Lean was not amused; he pulled out an envelope.

"Ah, Mr. Tube, it says here that you have a record of bad pranks. Now, if you feel like pulling another prank, I'll send you to the principal's office. Are we clear?" Everyone snickered as the young man's face turned red with embarrassment.

"Now who can tell me what ten and e equal?" continued Mr. Lean. No one raised their hand. Avery raised hers. "Yes, Miss Lawn, do you know the answer?" asked Mr. Lean.

"2.718281828459044," answered Avery with a smile.

"I'm sorry, Miss Lawn, but that's not the answer," said Mr. Lean.

"Huh!?" gasped Avery. "But I'm always right," she said, her face burning with embarrassment. The girl sat down in her chair and mumbled under her breath. Avery couldn't believe she had gotten the answer wrong. It never happened; she was always right with her math.

"Anyone know the answer?" asked Mr. Lean again. Angelina raised her hand. Avery had doubts that Angelina would get the answer right. She thought if she didn't know, then it wouldn't be Angelina. "Yes, Miss Golden?" said Mr. Lean.

"2.718281828459045," said Angelina.

"That is right," said Mr. Lean.

"What!?" exclaimed Avery, jumping out of her chair.

"I'm sorry, Ms. Lawn, but you were one-off," said Mr. Lean.

"But I know my math," said Avery. She felt a massive wave of embarrassment and confusion splash over her. Never had Avery gotten a question wrong, especially in front of the class. She wished Angelina had a different class.

CHAPTER THREE
DESTINY

"MAN, I HATE GETTING CRUSHED by the bigger kids!" complained one guy, sitting on the bench.

"Yeah, but at least some of them aren't here to crush us like bugs," said a second guy. They high-fived each other.

Angelina was tying her shoes when she saw her friends looking even worse than they were this morning.

"Do we really have to play dodgeball?" complained Leona.

"We always get crushed by the jocks anyways," whined Avery. Angelina walked over to them in hopes of cheering them up again.

"Come on, girls, nothing like a little exercise to get you ready for anything!" she cheered.

"Come on, people, let's hustle!" demanded Coach Joy. The kids ran and formed into two teams, boys and girls.

"Welcome back, everyone. I hope you had a good summer vacation. Alright, the rules are simple: grab a ball and hit someone. If you get hit, you're out," said the coach.

"Alright, let the game begin!" At the sound of her whistle, the game began.

A few people were already out as the game carried on, but some were just getting warmed up. Angelina was one of them. She was a pro. She was fast and quick on her feet, taking people out left and right.

"Wow, she's pretty good," said one guy.

"She's amazing!" said another girl from the bench.

"How is she so good?" asked Avery.

"I don't know, but she's crushing it," commented Leona. As the game continued, it was down to the final round, and only Angelina and Violet were left. The coach blew her whistle. Violet grabbed a ball and threw it hard at Angelina.

"LOOK OUT!" warned people on the bench. Angelina dodged the ball right as it was about to hit her. She picked up a ball and threw it at Violet.

"Uh, oh," whimpered Violet. She ran as fast as she could, but the ball hit her.

"Game! Angelina wins!" announced Coach Joy.

"WHAT!? NO!" shouted Violet.

"I'm sorry, miss Violet, but that's a game," said Coach Joy.

"But I always win!" complained Violet.

After P.E. ended, Angelina separated from her friends and caught up with Violet.

"Hey, Violet, good game," she said. She put out her hand for Violet to shake, but Violet laughed unpleasantly.

"Oh please, you're only saying that because you won. And even if you didn't win, I don't become friends with losers." Violet flipped her hair and sashayed off.

"I can't believe she beat Violet," said Leona.

"Yeah, we're usually the ones getting knocked out, and she shows us right off," said Avery.

"And she was always the star player," agreed Sophia.

Angelina walked over.

"What's next?"

"Lunch," said Avery.

They all walked into the cafeteria. Everyone sat down at a table while Angelina went in line to grab her lunch. When she picked up a tray, she noticed Max was in front of her.

"Hey!" said Angelina. Max turned around and smiled.

"Oh, hey!" said Max. The lunch lady grew impatient and told Max and Angelina to hurry up.

"Sorry," they said at the same time. They laughed and got their food.

"Seems like she's having a great first day," said Sophia, watching from her table.

"She's having a better day than me," said Avery with bitterness in her voice.

"Yeah, she's been a showoff all day," added Leona, filling with envy. They stopped talking when Angelina walked up to their table.

"Hey, guys, is it okay if I sit with you?" asked Angelina.

Sophia put her purse in the empty seat. "Sorry, we saved this seat for a girl we met," said Leona.

"Oh, okay," said Angelina, feeling a little disappointed, and she walked off to find another table.

"We should have let Angelina sit with us," said Avery, feeling a little guilty.

"She's fine," assured Leona. Angelina looked around for a table to sit at, but she was out of luck.

"Hey, Angelina!" called Max, waving. Angelina smiled as she noticed Max's invitation and walked over to the table. Violet caught her walking towards Max's table and smiled.

"It's payback time." She put out her glittery purple heel in front of Angelina. Angelina didn't notice Violet's heel and tripped.

Everything seemed to slow down as Angelina was about to become Violet's newest victim of humiliation. Angelina's necklace flared a golden light, and with it, a golden bubble wrapped around her tray before her face landed in it.

Silence spread through the whole cafeteria. Everyone took in what had just happened. Angelina froze in shock, trying to grab hold of everything. She slowly stood up and looked around to see people giving her strange stares and whispering to each other. Angelina looked at her necklace, held it in her hand, and ran out of the cafeteria.

"Angelina!" yelled Leona, Sophia, and Avery. They didn't know whether to run after her, so they stayed there confused.

***

ANGELINA RAN OUT OF THE SCHOOL. She didn't stop until she reached the backyard of the orphanage. She paused, gasping for air.

"What was that!?" she asked herself. Her necklace never did anything like that before, and why did it do it now? Was it telling her something she didn't know? Her head was flooded with confusion, fear, and shock. Angelina leaned up against a tree and sighed. "I don't understand. Why is this happening?" she asked. The girl held her necklace as she began to cry. She closed her eyes, letting the tears fall. But when she opened them, the tree she was leaning on was beaming with golden light.

"Hey, what's going on!?" yelled Angelina. The golden light pulled her in closer and closer. Angelina tried running away from the portal, but the force sucked her right in, and she was carried off.

CHAPTER FOUR
MAGICTOPIA

ANGELINA TRAVELED THROUGH a black hole. All she could see was pitch black, darkness. It felt as if she would forever be falling into the seemingly endless abyss. She spotted a bright light that got brighter as she fell further and further until she landed on a giant leaf leading to a huge tree branch. Angelina looked around. Everything was so beautiful, like something she would only see in a dream. The sky was a perfect blue with hints of yellow, seafoam green, and pink mixed in, with the golden sun's bright rays warming the magical land. The clouds looked like fluffy white pieces of cotton candy, and the leaf she was sitting on was an emerald green. And with the dewdrops on it, it truly did look like an emerald. She looked down. There were giant flowers, even more beautiful than any flower she had seen. Their petals seemed so soft, almost as if they were crafted out of silk, sparkling in the sun.

"Everything here is so beautiful!" gasped Angelina, soaking in the sight.

This place seemed so familiar… had she seen it before, maybe in her dreams? She destroyed the thought and continued on.

She tried climbing her way to the tree's branches, but she lost her grip and fell off. She screamed at the top of her lungs as she prayed not to fall to her death. Luckily, she landed in a giant pink flower.

"Woah, that was close," she sighed, catching her breath. She looked behind her. There were giant flowers in gold, pink, lavender, light green, icy blue, and red. She pushed the petal open, but there was nothing to stand on, and Angelina fell again.

"NOT AGAIN!" she screamed. As she came closer to the ground, she could see something that looked like a person standing right where she would land.

"LOOK OUT!" she called. The person looked up and moved out of the way. Angelina closed her eyes as she began to fall to her death. But just before she met her doom, her necklace glowed and caught her just inches off the ground. It lowered her down, and Angelina laid there, regaining her senses.

"Oh my goodness, are you okay?" asked a young girl around the same age as Angelina. She helped Angelina to her feet.

"Yea....yeah, I'm okay," answered Angelina.

As Angelina gained her sight, she took a moment to look at the young girl; there was something different about her. She had a slim hourglass figure, with cocoa brown skin and rosy cheeks. Her long, kinky rose hair was tied in a long side braid. She had pink eyes that reflected kindness and concern in them. She wore a pink plaid dress over a white short sleeve top with flats. The girl's blush pink wings sparkled in the sun and lightly fluttered. The girl examined Angelina too. She didn't have any pointed ears, wings, or any magical features; she just seemed like an ordinary being.

"Sorry, I've just never seen...anyone that looks like you," said Angelina, gazing at the girl's wings. "What are you, exactly?"

"I'm a fairy," the girl answered.

"A fairy..." Angelina repeated the words softly. "Where am I? What is this place?"

"This is Magictopia," the girl said, gesturing her arms open.

"Are there others that look like you?"

"Of course, there are fairies, elves, mermaids. All kinds of magical beings here."

"Woah," Angelina said, looking around at the new world she was now in.

She turned to the girl again.

"I'm sorry I haven't even introduced myself. I'm Angelina."

"I'm Ellie, and I've never seen a person without any magical features. Unless you have magical powers?"

"No," said Angelina. "I'm from a place called Earth, my necklace did some kind of magic, and it took me here."

Ellie's eyes opened wide.

"You're from Earth!? What's it like? Are you really a human!?" She questioned with excitement.

"Well…it's a planet without any magic… or like the magic here," said Angelina.

"Really!?" beamed Ellie. Angelina laughed at Ellie's excitement.

Well, since I'm here, I might as well make a friend, she thought.

The two began to walk as Angelina told Ellie all about Earth, what it was like, and all about humans.

CHAPTER FIVE
THE DARK QUEEN

FAR AWAY IN THE LAND LIVED the Dark Queen. She lived in a dark, tall, grim-looking castle; the area around it was ghastly and barren. In the watchtower were two elves watching over the land through telescopes.

"Find anything?" asked an elf.

"No, just two girls," replied another. He took a closer look at his telescope and studied Ellie and Angelina.

"No… no, it can't be… "

"What?" asked the first elf.

"One of those girls… she looks like… but it can't be," the second elf said astoundingly. The first elf looked through the telescope and gazed at Angelina. He studied her carefully from head to toe. He froze when he saw the necklace around her neck, and he held his breath.

"That…that girl… she's… "

"The lost princess!" The two elves exclaimed in unison. They bolted into the throne room, where the Dark Queen was sitting upon her great throne.

"*YOUR HIGHNESS! YOUR HIGHNESS!*" they yelled.

"What is it, you fools!?" hissed the Dark Queen. "Can't you see I'm busy!?"

The Dark Queen was a cold and dreadful woman. Her skin was dark brown; her eyes were like dark, cold pools of water that could even make a fearsome monster shiver in fear. An ink crown with dim colored gems was placed upon her long black ponytail. She wore a towering, tight, black dress with flowing, off-the-shoulder sleeves that showed off her slender frame. A running cape made of raven feathers was draped around her shoulders, covering the pitch-black feathered wings tucked behind her back.

"*WE FOUND HER, THE LOST PRINCESS!*" yelled the elves. The Dark Queen responded with a look of slight shock.

"Are you sure?" she asked.

"Yes, my queen, we just saw her. And there's no doubt it's her," said the first elf. The Queen stood up from her throne.

"Well, then let's give her a welcome gift she'll never forget." A wicked grin spread on her face.

She left the throne room and entered a room filled with a thousand monsters of all kinds. Some were big and some small. Some had long claws, while others had multiple heads. In one cage contained a giant rock monster. It let out a huge, thunderous roar.

"Now that's the kind of energy you use on the battlefield," said the Dark Queen. "I want you to find the lost princess and destroy her once and for all."

The monster broke open the bars of its cage with its bare hands, jumping out the window and beginning its hunt for the girls. The queen watched the beast with satisfaction and headed back to her throne.

She stopped when a young girl stepped in front of her.

"Angela!" yelled the queen. She was so shocked she jumped.

"Mother, what's going on?" asked the girl.

The girl was fourteen. She wore black glasses over her dark brown eyes that glistened like rich honey under the light. A silver tiara encrusted with dark stones was placed over the black curls that she kept in a neat bun. Her smooth skin was a chocolate complexion. Her dress was a similar style as her mother's, except it was dark silver, with dark silky patterns and puffy sleeves.

"Everything's fine, dear. I'm just settling some business," said the queen. The tone of her voice changed from cruel and sharp to kind and motherly.

"There's nothing to worry about, sweetie. Just go back to your room, okay?" She put her hand on Angela's cheek.

"Alright, mother," obeyed Angela. She turned around and headed back to her room. The Dark Queen wiped the sweet smile off her face as soon as she saw Angela out of her sight. She went back into the throne room and sat at her dark throne, waiting for the news of the two girls' death.

CHAPTER SIX
DISCOVERY

ANGELINA AND ELLIE were still on their walk, getting to know one another, not aware of the imminent danger. They enjoyed their conversation and each other's company until the monster jumped in front of them, letting out a huge roar.

"Woah, what is that!?" yelled Angelina.

"I think it's a rock monster!" said Ellie.

The monster let out another roar before slamming its fist down at them. The girls bolted in separate directions, nearly missing the giant hand. The beast turned to Angelina and threw its massive fist at her. Angelina jumped and ducked, barely missing the monster's fist by a mere fraction. The beast turned its attention to Ellie and tried to catch the fairy. Ellie took to the sky, spinning and fluttering to escape the creature's grasp. The monster then began to throw huge rocks at them.

"Look out!" warned Angelina.

The two girls jumped seconds before an incoming rock could hit them. The monster continued to throw rocks at them.

"Where'd it even come from?!" yelled Ellie.

"I have no idea!" Angelina yelled back.

Soon the monster became impatient and slammed its foot on the ground, making the floor quake and opening cracks in the dirt. The girls ran as the cracks widened. Their hearts boomed while they raced as fast as they could. Ellie came to a sudden halt when she saw her foot was jammed in the cracks. She tried to pull herself out, but it didn't work. Angelina stopped and ran back to help her friend.

"Hang on, I'm coming!" she called.

They tried with all their might and strength to get Ellie out, but it was no use. The monster caught the eye of the girls and walked over to them. Angelina and Ellie hurried once more to free Ellie before the monster reached them. But the beast had already contacted them and aimed its fist right at them.

The girls held each other tight, knowing their fates were sealed. The creature then slammed its fist at them.

They shut their eyes.

All time seemed to have slowed down, and the end was near…when a golden shield appeared out of Angelina's necklace, just as the monster was about to hit them.

When the beast hit the shield, it crumbled into a vast pile of rocks.

There was a moment of silence as the girls slowly opened their eyes and looked at what used to be the monster.

Ellie was finally able to free her foot, and the two girls stood there, in silence, trying to take in what had just happened. The silence was broken when Ellie began to speak.

"That…was…INCREDIBLE!" Ellie exclaimed. Angelina laughed nervously.

"Yeah…it was." She felt a little dizzy after what just happened.

Ellie suddenly eyed her with suspension.

"What is it?" asked Angelina.

"Wait, you're from Earth, right?" asked Ellie.

"Yes," said Angelina, a little confused at what Ellie was getting at.

"And you had that necklace for how long?"

"Ever since I was a baby."

"And it made a shield?"

"And a bubble," added Angelina. Ellie paused for a moment, thinking about something. A smile slowly came on her face. She turned to Angelina, with her eyes beaming with joy.

"You're the lost princess!" she exclaimed.

"The lost…what?" asked Angelina with a puzzled look.

"The lost princess!" repeated Ellie. "It's the story of the angel Queen sending her daughter to Earth to save her from the Dark Queen."

"Sounds like an epic story," said Angelina.

"It is!" said Ellie. "It's in the origin book at the library."

With that, Ellie grabbed Angelina by her wrist, and the two began their journey, with excitement buzzing through their veins.

CHAPTER SEVEN
REBECCA

THE TWO ELVES IN THE WATCHTOWER watched as the girls continued on their journey.

"The queen's not going to like this," said the first elf. They slowly approached the throne room and kneeled before the queen.

"Um, your… highness… we have some news," whimpered the first elf.

"What is it now?" the Dark Queen asked, annoyed.

"There's something…Rob wanted to say to you!"

"WHAT!?" shouted the second elf.

"Well, Rob, what is it?" asked the Dark Queen impatiently.

"Well… the… princess… is not… dead."

"WHAT DO YOU MEAN SHE'S NOT DEAD!?" yelled the queen, standing from her throne.

"Well, you see… my queen. The girl's necklace saved her and her friend," said the first elf.

"I should've never sent that worthless monster in the first place!" She grumbled. She turned back to the first elf.

"Roger, go get Rebecca," she ordered the little elf.

"Yes, ma'am!" said the elf. He left the throne room and entered a vast, dark place, weapons hanging from the walls. There in the room was a woman practicing her dark magic. The woman was a pale and slender figure. She had short, black hair and cold grey eyes filled with hate. She wore a long white dress with a symbol of a broken heart with black ooze pouring out and long black gloves.

"Rebecca, element of hate," said the elf.

"What is it?" asked Rebecca, annoyed to be interrupted from her training.

"The Dark Queen requests you," said the elf.

Rebecca followed him into the throne room.

"You requested me, my queen?" she asked, kneeling before her.

The Dark Queen stood up from her throne.

"Yes, I have summoned you with a mission to complete. It seems that the lost princess is still alive after all these years and has returned. I want you to find her and her fairy friend and end their lives," she said coldly. Rebecca smiled maliciously.

"Do you think you can handle it?" asked the Dark Queen.

"Oh my queen, I've been waiting for this moment for a long time," said Rebecca. She disappeared in a cloud of dark smoke and began her search for the girls.

"My queen, are you sure she can do it?" asked one of the elves.

"Trust me, Roger, no one can beat the elements of destruction."

CHAPTER EIGHT
THE TALE OF THE LOST PRINCESS

ANGELINA AND ELLIE ENTERED THE LIBRARY and walked to the front desk.

"Excuse me, Mrs. Slug?" said Ellie, looking around for someone to answer. An elderly woman slowly came to the desk. Angelina took a closer look at her. She had big orange snail eyes and a giant yellow snail shell on her back. Angelina gasped at the sight of her.

"Hello, dear, how may I help you?" asked the woman.

"We're looking for the copy of the Magictopian origin book. Do you know where we can find it?"

"It should be down there. You can't miss it," said Mrs. Slug, smiling.

"Thank you," said Ellie.

The girls walked down the great library. It was filled with millions of books. Each one had a magnificent cover and looked great to read.

They stopped in front of a high marble shelf.

"There it is!" said Ellie.

She flew up and grabbed the book. It was the most beautiful novel they had ever seen. It was a giant thick book; the cover was a mix of gold, pink, lavender, green, red, and icy blue.

The History of Magictopia sparkled in gold.

"That's the origin book. It tells all of Magictopia's history, beings, and lands," explained Ellie.

"It's beautiful," said Angelina.

They sat down at a table, opened the book, and began to read.

"Millions of years ago, the angels created and ruled a beautiful, magical land called Magictopia. They used the elements of creation-- light, love, water, nature, ice, and fire-- to make and protect the planet. They had magical jewelry to transform and use their weapons to fight."

"Wow, that's amazing," sighed Angelina.

"Now, let me tell you the story of the angel queen," said Ellie.

She flipped the pages and stopped at a different chapter.

"Fourteen years ago, Magictopia was ruled by a kind and noble queen, but the queen's twin sister's jealousy got the best of her, and she attacked. Luckily, the queen defeated her, but soon her sister came back and got revenge by killing her sister and her human husband."

"Wait, human husband?" asked Angelina.

"Yes, the queen married a human, and they had two daughters," Ellie explained. "But the Dark Queen killed one of them and the king. The queen was able to send her other daughter to Earth before the Dark Queen could kill her."

Angelina looked at the pictures of the book. There the angel queen was holding a baby in her arms. She touched the picture and held her necklace.

"I-I'm…a princess," she whispered. She smiled and stood on the chair. "I'm a princess!" she announced. "Do you hear me? I'm a princess!"

"Shhh!" shushed Mrs. Slug.

"Sorry," apologized Angelina. She sat back in her chair and looked at her hands. She could feel the magic that was flowing in her veins.

"Come on, let's go so you can celebrate somewhere else," said Ellie, teasing her new friend. They left the table and headed to the librarian's desk.

"Did you find what you need?" asked Mrs. Slug.

"Yes, thank you, Mrs. Slug," said Ellie. She handed Mrs. Slug the book, and she opened it and stamped it. Nothing happened.

"Huh?" asked Angelina. She wondered why nothing showed. When pink glitter words appeared magically, they said, "Please return in 23 days." Angelina was amazed by the magical words as Mrs. Slug handed Ellie the book back.

"Thanks, Mrs. Slug!" commented Ellie as she and Angelina walked out of the library.

As they headed on their way, Rebecca landed right in front of them.

She gave them an evil grin.

"Well, well, well. If it isn't the lost princess. It seems that the stories were true," She said, eyeing Angelina.

Angelina stepped in front of Ellie.

"Who are you, and what do you want?" she demanded in a harsh voice.

"Oh, nothing, just to do what I came for. To destroy you!" said Rebecca. She blasted a dark beam of magic at the girls, and Angelina pushed Ellie out of the way. Rebecca continued to attack them, then fired one at Angelina. She jumped out of the way. Rebecca shot a few more at Angelina and another at Ellie. The girls ran, dodging the dark orbs. Rebecca turned her attention to Ellie, blasting a black beam at her. The beam missed Ellie, and it aimed at where a mother and daughter with butterfly wings froze, watching in fear as it headed straight at them. Ellie and Angelina spotted them and ran over to them.

"Hang on, we're coming!" said Ellie. They jumped, pushing the daughter and mother out of the way in different directions. Rebecca smiled as she saw her chance.

"Well, I was planning on destroying the princess. But, I want to get rid of you first!" said Rebecca.

She aimed her hand at Ellie and blasted a dark beam. Ellie pushed the girl out of the way before the beam hit her.

"Ellie!" shouted Angelina. She tried to run to Ellie, but it was too late. The mother and daughter ran from the battle. There was nothing but black smoke and silence. "Ellie," she cried. Angelina collapsed to the floor as her heart sank. She had lost her only friend in this world. Tears began to fill her eyes. But as the smoke cleared, Ellie appeared! She had a pink bracelet on her wrist, with shimmering pink gems.

"Ellie!" cheered Angelina.

"*WHAT!?*" yelled Rebecca. She noticed the bracelet on Ellie's wrist and boiled with anger.

"If you think for a second, you can beat me now that you've found the second element, think again!" She blasted another dark orb at the girls. Angelina pulled out her shield while Ellie studied her new bracelet.

"Where did this come from? And why do I have it?" questioned Ellie. She touched the jewelry and shook it to see if anything would happen. A pink bow and arrow appeared in her hands.

"W...what?" Ellie turned to the battle between Angelina and Rebecca. She tried aiming and shooting her arrow and missed.

"Ha! You call yourself the element of love? You don't even know how to use your own weapon!" mocked Rebecca. Angelina tossed her shield, hitting Rebecca's head.

"Hey! Don't talk about my friend like that!" Ellie tried again with her arrow. She aimed, and it grazed Rebecca.

"Nice work Ellie!" complimented Angelina.

"You little pests!" growled Rebecca. She blasted a giant orb at Ellie, but she flew out of the way. Rebecca began firing huge powerful balls at her. Angelina hit Rebecca with her shield again, making Rebecca direct her attacks to Angelina. Rebecca shot a colossal blast of dark magic at Angelina. Angelina put up her cover, and she used all her strength to push back the magic while Rebecca was pushing her magic against Angelina. Ellie helped Angelina fight back the magic, using all their might. That was when Angelina's necklace glowed and gave her the strength to push back the magic. Rebecca was too late to avoid the hit, and it blasted her so far until she was out of sight. Angelina and Ellie fell to the ground as they gasped for air.

"Who was that?" asked Angelina.

"I don't know… maybe she was sent by the Dark Queen," suggested Ellie. Angelina stood up and helped Ellie to her feet.

"Well, at least she's gone. That was some awesome teamwork back there," said Angelina, trying to brighten the mood. She raised her hand for a high-five. Ellie gave her a confused look.

"Oh, I guess you don't know that," said Angelina, lowering her hand.

"Hey, while you're here, you might as well teach me a little about Earth," said Ellie. Angelina raised her hand, and Ellie high-fived her. Angelina noticed the bracelet on Ellie.

"Where'd that come from?" she asked.

"I have no idea; it just appeared in the middle of the battle," responded Ellie.

"Huh, that's strange."

"So, what do we do now?"

"Well, there's no doubt that the Dark Queen knows about us."

"We have to stay low until we figure out our next plan of action."

"The only way we can defend ourselves from the Dark Queen is if we gather the elements like the book said," Angelina explained.

"You're right, and maybe we can figure out what this bracelet is for," agreed Ellie. "Well, we better go. I'm tired, anyway. Since you don't have anywhere to go, you can stay with me."

"Really? Thank you," said Angelina gratefully. Then, they began heading towards Ellie's house. They stopped when they reached a small, rose-colored home with beautiful roses planted in the grass. Ellie pulled out a key from her pocket and opened the door. As they walked into the house, Angelina looked around. The place gave a feeling of safety and comfort. It was colored with shades of pink, purple, and white.

"Wow, this is a charming house," Angelina said.

"Thank you," said Ellie.

"Do you live here by yourself?" asked Angelina, seeing no sign of anyone else.

"Yes, ever since the Dark Queen attacked, people of Magictopia trained their children to be strong enough to defend themselves," explained Ellie.

Man, Ms. A wouldn't even let me be out past nine, thought Angelina.

After Ellie gave her a tour of the house, she led her to a small, pink room with a bed, dresser, and nightstand.

"Here you go," said Ellie.

"Thank you, I couldn't be any more grateful," said Angelina.

"Of course, I can't let my new friend find somewhere to sleep on her own," said Ellie.

She left the room to let Angelina settle herself. Angelina walked in, put her hat on the dresser, took off her shoes, and laid on the bed. She looked at her necklace; it was a golden heart locket with diamonds and golden angel wings attached. She remembered when Ms. A gave it to her.

This is the necklace you had when you were dropped off at the orphanage. She remembered her kind voice. It all felt like a dream—her, a princess? She had always thought of the possibility of coming from royalty or some wealthy family, but she would never have thought that she was a half-angel who was the next ruler and protector of her land, which she now had to free. It all felt like a crazy dream that she couldn't wake up from, and everything she thought was a lie.

She was glad she had met Ellie and that she didn't have to do this alone. At least she had someone to lean on and understood what it was like to have your world turn upside down. She held onto her necklace as she closed her eyes and fell asleep as a mixture of excitement, fear, and shock filled in her mind.

CHAPTER NINE
AQUARIUS

THE SUN ROSE, and the golden light shined on Angelina's face, waking her up. Looking out the window, it was about seven o'clock. She rubbed her tired eyes and went into the kitchen. She grabbed some eggs from the cabinets and began cooking. Ellie came, with the origin book in her hands, and sat at the table.

"Good morning," said Angelina.

"Good morning," replied Ellie.

"I see you brought the book," said Angelina.

"Yeah, I was doing some reading last night," said Ellie. Angelina set a plate of eggs in front of her, and Ellie took a bite.

"Mm. Delicious," complimented Ellie.

"Thanks. I grew up in an orphanage, and Ms. A taught us how to cook," said Angelina.

"Who's Ms. A?" asked Ellie.

"Ms. A was the owner of the orphanage I lived in. She's like a mother to me," explained Angelina. She began to feel sad thinking about her old home and tried to change the subject.

"So, where do we go if you find the element of water?" she asked.

Ellie opened the origin book and showed a map of Magictopia. It was filled with lands from the cold Winters' Forest to the Fire Grounds. The Rocky Caverns and Astral Realm were shown high in the skies and low grounds of Magictopia.

"If the next element is water, then we should go to The Crystal Water Ocean," said Ellie.

"Alright then! After breakfast, we're off to the Crystal Water Ocean," announced Angelina. The two ate their breakfast, packed, and headed out to find the third element.

***

MEANWHILE, at the castle, the Dark Queen was stomping back and forth with fury.

"*I CAN'T BELIEVE YOU DIDN'T KILL THOSE BRATS!*" she yelled.

"I'm sorry, my queen; I'll prove myself once again. I promise," said Rebecca, with her head down in shame.

"You've failed once: unless you can prove yourself powerful, you are not needed," said the Dark Queen. Rebecca left the room, and the Dark Queen sat on her throne.

"Roger, go get Aquarius," she commanded.

"Yes, ma'am!" said the elf. He marched off and went into a room with a pool full of dark water. Swimming in the pool was a water fairy.

"Aquarius, element of dark water," announced the elf. The fairy got out of the water.

"Yes?" she asked, draining the water out of her long, thin, dark blue hair. She was a small woman with an hourglass figure, her skin was cornflower blue, and her navy blue eyes were filled with vanity. Her dark wings shimmered with the water dripping from them. She wore a long, dark off-the-shoulder aqua dress, with a split, in the end, showing off her long legs. She wore matching boots and a dark choker with a sapphire around it.

"Your mission is to destroy the lost princess and the element of love before they find the water element," said the elf.

"Finally, something to do," said Aquarius. Water emerged from the pool and began to circle her. It swirled faster and faster until Aquarius disappeared, off to the Crystal Ocean.

***

ANGELINA AND ELLIE ARRIVED AT THE CRYSTAL OCEAN. It was a beautiful sight. The water was clear, and it sparkled under the light of the golden sun. The sand was soft, and huge rocks crowded near the water.

"Okay, let's split-up. I think we might find the third element that way," suggested Angelina.

"Okay," said Ellie. They went in separate ways. Angelina went near an area with pools of water surrounded by rocks.

"Now, let's see. Where would the element of water be?" Angelina asked herself. Her necklace glowed, and a golden speck of light flew off.

Angelina followed the trace. It took her to the ocean and dove in the water. Angelina stopped in front of the water and lowered her head over it. She thought she saw something moving in there, maybe a person.

"Hello?" asked Angelina. "Is anyone there?" Nothing happened. Angelina stood there as what she thought she saw earlier came closer and closer. Fearing another one of the Dark Queen's monsters to attack, she pulled out her shield and prepared for whatever it was to come out. The figure emerged from the water. It was a mermaid who seemed to be the same age as Angelina. Her face was filled with worry. Angelina lowered her shield to examine her.

The girl had had a pear-shaped figure with periwinkle skin, and her lavender eyes were like shimmering pearls. Her long lilac hair was tied in a ponytail that reached all the way down to her behind. Her matching mermaid tail glistened under the sunlight, nearly blinding Angelina with its beauty. Gills striped both sides of her neck and hips. She wore a beautiful lavender head chain, pearls sparkling from it.

"Um...hello?" said Angelina cautiously. The girl turned to Angelina and gave her a small smile.

"Hello, I'm Angelina," introduced Angelina with a friendly smile.

"I'm Opal," said the mermaid. The two shook hands.

"I have another friend with me; she'd love to meet you," said Angelina. She stood up and faced Ellie.

"Hey, Ellie! I think I found something!" She called. The fairy ran over to them.

"Did you find the third element?" she asked. She moved her eyes to Opal, and she smiled at her.

"This is Opal. I just met her," explained Angelina.

"Hi, I'm Ellie," said Ellie, putting out her hand.

"I'm Opal," said Opal as she shook Ellie's hand.

"So, what brings you here?" asked Ellie. Opal's face turned sad.

"Someone has been destroying our kingdom. I came here to find someone to help me," Opal explained.

"Wow, I'm sorry," pitied Angelina.

Ellie lightly grabbed Angelina's arm. "Can we talk for a moment?" she whispered.

Angelina turned to Opal.

"Um. Will you excuse us for a minute?" asked Angelina. The two moved away from Opal.

"I know she needs our help, but how can we know she's telling the truth?" asked Ellie. "She could be lying."

"You're right. She might be one of the Dark Queen's traps," Angelina agreed. They turned to Opal, eyeing her with slight suspicion and unsure of what to do.

Angelina's necklace glowed, and a golden speck of light appeared, spinning around Opal.

"The necklace must be saying she's telling the truth," said Angelina.

"And that she must have the element of water," said Ellie. They walked back to Opal.

"Opal, we'll help you find the person behind destroying your kingdom," said Angelina.

"Really? Thank you!" said Opal with a bright smile.

"But how can we help you? We can't breathe underwater," Ellie pointed out.

"I've got it!" said Opal. Her headpiece glowed, and magic circled Angelina's and Ellie's legs. It gave Angelina a golden mermaid tail and Ellie a pink one. Then the magic moved towards their heads, which gave them gills to breathe.

"This is awesome!" said Angelina.

"Beautiful!" gushed Ellie.

They dived into the water and looked around. There were beautifully detailed buildings, some crushed and destroyed, with pieces falling to the seafloor.

"Looks like the culprit sure made a mess of things," said Angelina.

"*OPAL CRYSTAL PEARL! WHERE HAVE YOU BEEN!?*" boomed a voice. It was the king of the Crystal Water Ocean, swimming over to Opal.

"Father, I came to find some help, and these two offered to help us," Opal said, pointing to Ellie and Angelina.

"*WHAT!? YOU BROUGHT TWO STRANGERS WITH YOU!?*" boomed the king.

"But father, they offered to help us. And I think this girl is the lost princess, see her necklace?" she said, pointing to Angelina.

"*OH, PLEASE! THE LOST PRINCESS HASN'T BEEN FOUND FOR YEARS!*"

Angelina swam up to the king and bowed.

"Your highness, I know this is hard to believe, but your daughter's right. I'm the lost princess." Angelina's necklace glowed brightly, its magic swirling.

"Well, it looks like my daughter is telling the truth," said the king, finally calm. "Do you think you can help us? Someone has destroyed our homes, and we don't know who or how to stop them."

"Don't worry, your highness, we'll stop them!" assured Angelina. Angelina, Ellie, and Opal swam off to find the culprit. They looked around for clues that could lead them to who was behind this.

"Hey, look," said Opal, pointing. "It's a trail of ink."

"Maybe it'll lead us to the person behind all of this," suggested Ellie. They followed the trail. It took them far, through the ocean.

They stopped when they saw it lead to land.

"Huh?" asked Ellie.

"It looks like we're going up," said Angelina. They swam up to land. Angelina and Ellie jumped out of the water, their mermaid tails disappearing and their legs reappearing. They gave a confused look when they saw that the trail was cut off, and there weren't any other clues leading to the culprit.

"I don't get it," said Angelina. "Why did the trail just cut off like that?"

Suddenly, the air was filled with a wicked laugh, and Aquarius emerged from the water.

"Well now, if it isn't the lost princess and element of love," she said, looking at Angelina and Ellie.

"Wait, you're the one that's been destroying my kingdom!?" exclaimed Opal, burning with fury.

"Of course, it was all part of my plan to send you all on a wild goose chase and trap you!" explained Aquarius, flashing Opal an evil grin. Angelina and Ellie stepped in front of Opal.

"Stand back," warned Angelina.

She pulled out her shield while Ellie got out her bow and arrow. Aquarius raised her arms, water emerging from the water and forming eight tentacles.

They charged at Aquarius, and Ellie shot an arrow at one of her limbs. Aquarius flicked away the shaft, throwing one of her limbs at Ellie.

Angelina jumped in front of Ellie, pushing back Aquarius's hit.

"This will be easier than I thought! Perhaps I gave you too much credit!" taunted Aquarius.

She raised two tentacles, slamming them down at Angelina and Ellie. The girls ran from the attack as they tried fending off the arm. Angelina put up her shield. A tentacle came crashing down on her, pushing her hard to the ground.

"I don't think this is working," said Ellie, shooting another arrow.

"Maybe we need to transform," suggested Angelina.

"How do we do that?" asked Ellie.

"I don't know, just...try!" yelled Angelina. She used all her strength as a tentacle kept hitting her shield.

"Transform?" said Ellie.

"Abracadabra?" blurted Angelina. They ran and hid behind a huge rock. Ellie continued to shoot her arrows while Angelina sat there, her mind in a panic.

Come on, Angelina, what would you say to transform? she thought frantically. She took a deep breath and held her necklace. "Angelina, element of light!" she yelled.

Angelina's necklace glowed and lifted her in the air.

"Uh....what's happening!?" panicked Angelina.

Golden magic emerged from her necklace and swirled around her hair, tying it in an elegant bun.

The light went down to her body, replacing her clothes with a long, beautiful, golden dress with a slit at the bottom.

The dress was completed with golden gloves and high heeled boots. More magic smoothed on her eyelids and lips, giving her golden eyeshadow and red lipstick.

Angelina lowered to the ground. She gazed at her new outfit.

She looked just like a princess.

"Wow, I can't believe it," she thought in amazement. She spun gracefully in her new dress.

"My turn!" said Ellie. "Ellie, element of love!"

She was lifted into the air. Pink magic from her bracelet loosened her side braid, giving her a half ponytail style. The magic swirled her body, replacing her clothes with a sleeveless, pink top and a matching, puffy, flowery bottom. She was finished off with matching gloves and heels. Pink eyeshadow and lipstick appeared on her face.

Ellie pulled out her bow and arrow as she landed back to the ground. She looked at her magical dress and carefully touched her hair.

"I... can't believe it..." she awed.

"Ellie, you look great!" beamed Angelina.

"Your pretty little dresses aren't going to stop me!" interrupted Aquarius.

She darted more tentacles at them. Angelina and Ellie avoided them. Ellie flew in the air while Angelina attacked from the ground. Angelina shot beams of light at the tentacles as she jumped and dodged Aquarius's strikes.

"I think I'm getting the hang of this," said Angelina. Ellie blasted her arrows. Aquarius aimed three tentacles at her. Ellie flew as fast as she could as the tentacles were right on her tail. She turned around and shot a giant arrow at them; the tentacles dissolved into water. Aquarius growled, pulling another limb at Ellie. Ellie flew past the attack and shot an arrow at Aquarius, blazing her shoulder, making it bleed.

"That's it!" yelled Aquarius. She picked up Angelina and Ellie with her tentacles, coiling tightly around them, slowly crushing them.

"You thought you were so clever, didn't you?" mocked Aquarius. She watched with glee as the girls gasped for air, and their faces turned pale.

"Soon, the lost princess will be gone this time!" Aquarius stopped when she felt something hit the back of her head. She slowly turned around as she held the shell that hit her.

"Who is responsible for that!?" she demanded.

"I am!" yelled a voice. Aquarius turned around. There was Opal, had with an arm full of seashells.

"Opal!" yelled Angelina and Ellie.

"And who do you think you are!?" demanded Aquarius.

"Opal Crystal Pearl! Princess of the Crystal Water Ocean, and I will not let you hurt my friends!" announced Opal. She threw another shell at Aquarius, but Aquarius smacked it away with her tentacle. The tentacle came darting at Opal.

"Opal!" cried Ellie and Angelina. They used all their might to free themselves and save her, yet it was hopeless.

Opal froze in fear as the tentacle came flying at her until her head chain began to glow and stopped Aquarius's attack.

"What's happening!?" gasped Aquarius, shocked. The light dissolved the tentacle and lifted her into the air. A bright gleam emerged from the chain, sweeping through Opal's hair, giving her a braided ponytail decorated with pearl beads. The light swirled around her body. A long-sleeved, shimmering lavender-colored dress with a long lace train appeared with knee-high amethyst colored boots.

A lavender gem whip appeared, and her tail turned into two legs. Opal came to the ground and wobbled.

"Opal, you're the element of water!" said Angelina.

Aquarius boiled in anger, creating two more tentacles while pushing Angelina and Ellie aside, who were still stuck in Aquarius's trap. Aquarius darted a tentacle at Opal, and Opal wobbled as she dodged it.

She looked around and looked at the ocean, an idea popping in her mind. She jumped in the water with her head chain glowing and created lavender water tentacles of her own.

Aquarius shot more tentacles at Opal. Opal blocked them with hers. Aquarius pushed her back and punched her before she could get up.

"Opal!" cried Angelina and Ellie. They struggled to try to free themselves from Aquarius's grip. Aquarius grabbed Opal by a tentacle and laughed.

"It was so sweet of you to try to save your friends, even when you couldn't even save yourself," she mocked.

She grinned as she slowly crushed Opal. Opal gasped for air as she tried to escape from Aquarius's grip. Her eyesight was slowly fading; she knew she was reaching closer to her end. Opal used the last bit of her energy to raise her arm; the water from the ocean slowly formed into a tentacle.

The tentacle rose from the water and punched Aquarius. Aquarius lost her grip on Opal. Opal jumped back into the water and hit her again. Aquarius formed even more tentacles, striking them on Opal.

Opal fought back, and soon, the two were throwing hits back and forth. Opal was getting the upper hand on Aquarius until Aquarius grabbed her tentacles and began pushing her down.

"HA! DID YOU HONESTLY THINK YOU COULD DEFEAT ME? It's about time I put you in your place!" she mocked.

Opal used all her might pushing back while she thought of ways she could defeat Aquarius. She closed her eyes and focused all her strength, wishing for something to happen.

Suddenly her head chain glowed, filling her with strength. She pushed Aquarius off her and gave her a few hard hits before she could get up. While Aquarius was still down, Opal wrapped her around her tentacles, causing her to free Angelina and Ellie and began spinning. She spun faster and faster until she threw her into the air. Opal finished Aquarius off by hitting her with a final punch, watching her blast off out of sight.

Opal's tentacles deformed back to water, and she was lowered back to the ground. Angelina and Ellie ran to Opal's side.

"Opal! Are you okay!?" asked Ellie. Opal took a few deep breaths and smiled at Ellie.

"Yeah, I'm just glad you guys are okay." Ellie and Angelina gave Opal a huge hug.

"Opal," called a voice from behind. They turned around. It was Opal's father.

"Uh, girls, I need a moment with my father," said Opal.

"Of course," said Angelina. Opal walked over to her father, sitting in front of him.

"Father, I know you may think I'm young and that I might not be ready for this responsibility." She began. "But, I was chosen to save our people from the evil it's facing. This is something I just have to do." She looked her father straight in the eyes showing she was serious. The king sighed as he looked at his daughter with gentle eyes.

"Opal, the moment I held you in my arms, I promised that harm would never come to you. And I always knew that you would do great things. And... I can't stop you from your destiny," he said. "Just promise me that you'll be safe."

"Of course, father," said Opal. She gave her father a long goodbye hug before getting up and walking off. She stopped and watched as he dove back into the water. Angelina and Ellie went up to her.

"You okay?" asked Angelina, patting her back.

"Yeah, I'm fine," said Opal, wiping a tear from her cheek. Angelina and Ellie helped her to her feet as she held onto them on the way to Ellie's home.

When they arrived, they went inside, and Ellie greeted Opal to her home.

"Welcome to my home!" she said with a welcoming smile.

"You have such a nice house," complemented Opal.

"Thank you," said Ellie. After Ellie showed her around, she led her into a room with light amethyst walls, a bed, and a dresser.

"This will be your new room," said Ellie. Opal thanked Ellie and went in and got settled. Later that night, Angelina laid on her bed with the thought of what the other elements would be like.

Wonder where to meet them next, she thought. She turned off the lights and went to sleep.

CHAPTER TEN
FARMER'S MARKET

ANGELINA WOKE UP early once again. She met up with Opal and Ellie in the kitchen.

"So, where should we find the fourth element?" asked Angelina.

"Actually, it looks like we're going to have to go to the market," said Ellie, closing the empty cabinets.

"But, we still need to find the fourth element," reminded Opal.

"Hey, maybe my necklace can help us," suggested Angelina. She put her hand on her necklace and closed her eyes. The locket filled the room with golden light, nearly blinding Ellie and Opal. Then it suddenly stopped. Angelina opened her eyes and looked at her necklace.

"Huh, I thought it would do more than-" The necklace dragged her towards the door.

"Hey! What's happening!?" asked Angelina. Ellie and Opal ran and pulled her back. But the necklace pulled Angelina out of their grip, opening the door and dragging her out.

"Woah!" yelled Angelina.

"Don't worry, we're right behind you!" called Ellie. She and Opal ran after Angelina. The necklace pulled Angelina before suddenly stopping in front of a small white cottage. There were barrels and baskets filled with fruits, vegetables, herbs, and other plants.

"Good morning, I'm April; how may I help you today?" greeted a nature elf.

The elf had a petite and shorter frame to her. She had long, straight, red hair that reached down to her back, and her skin was a peach tone. She gave off the feeling of comfort and warmth with her soft smile and delicate light green eyes. Her outfit was a white floral patterned dress that reached down to her knees, completed with sandals. Freckles danced across her gentle face.   Opal and Ellie came jogging, breathlessly, towards them.

"There… you are," gasped Ellie.

"We…thought we lost… you," Opal sighed, falling to her knees, taking deep breaths.

"Are you okay?" asked April.

"They're fine; they just went for a run," said Angelina. After they caught their breath, they stood close to Angelina.

"We better keep an eye out; you never know when the Dark Queen's demons might come back," warned Angelina.

***

BACK AT THE CASTLE, the Dark Queen sat on her throne, anger boiling over her until she couldn't contain it any longer.

"I CAN'T BELIEVE YOU STILL HAVEN'T GOTTEN RID OF THEM, AND NOW THEY'RE CLOSER TO FINDING THE REST OF THE ELEMENTS!" she screamed.

"I'm sorry, my queen, but I didn't think they would be so powerful," whimpered Aquarius, kneeling on the floor.

"WHAT DO YOU MEAN THEY'RE POWERFUL!? THEY JUST DISCOVERED THEIR POWERS; IT SHOULD'VE BEEN AN EASY TARGET!" The Dark Queen yelled at the top of her lungs. She took a deep breath, finally calming herself.

"Leave, you are no longer needed," she said to Aquarius. Aquarius left the room; one of the elf guards walked in.

"My queen, do you need me to get the other elements?" he asked.

"No, not yet anyway. The elements of creation have proven to be stronger each time we attack," The Dark Queen said. "Besides, I need time to think of a plan that will finally end them once and for all."

She left the throne room as she began to create a new plan to defeat the elements of creation.

***

THE ELEMENTS were still in April's market, buying their food.

"The necklace leads us all the way here, and we still haven't found the fourth element," whispered Angelina to Ellie.

"I know," agreed Ellie.

"Did you say something?" asked April.

"Oh, uh...we were just saying what a good day it is," said Angelina. April handed their things in a wooden basket, and Ellie gave her twenty gold coins.

"Have a nice day," said April, waving goodbye.

"Thanks, you too," waved back Opal. The girls began to walk away when they heard a loud crash.

"What was that!?" startled Ellie. They all ran to where the noise was coming from. They stopped in front of a tree that had been struck in half.

"What happened!?" asked Angelina.

"It looks like something, or someone, hit this tree in half," said Ellie.

"Whatever it was, it wasn't an accident."

"Why would someone do something to one of nature's beautiful creations?" asked April pitifully. A little white bunny came hopping along when a huge branch fell from the tree and came ready to crash down on the rabbit.

"Don't worry, little guy. I'll save you!" said April. She ran over and grabbed the bunny at the last minute. The branch came crashing down on her.

April put her arm over her head. A silver, wooden staff with green vines wrapped around it appeared in her hand, crushing the branch before it could hit April and the rabbit. Green emerald earrings flashed on April's pointed ears. She put the rabbit down and watched it hop along. Angelina, Ellie, and Opal ran to her. "What just happened?" asked April, stunned while standing to her feet. She looked at the staff with a confused and shocked look.

"What is this?" she asked gasping.

Angelina put her hand on April's shoulder.

"Look, I know this may sound crazy, but we're the elements of creation. And you've been chosen as the element of nature," explained Angelina.

April only looked at her as if she was crazy until she looked at her staff and Angelina's necklace.

"So, that means… you're the lost princess," she said, gazing at Angelina.

"And…I'm the element of nature…" Her voice was soft and filled with amazement.

"Yeah, isn't that amazing?" said Opal, cheerfully.

"So what happens now?" asked April.

"Well, you'll have to come with us, especially since the Dark Queen knows about us," said Ellie.

"Okay, but let me get my things first, if I may," said April.

"Of course," said Ellie. April ran into her house and came back out five minutes later, with a small bag.

"I'm ready," said April.

The sun began to set by the time the girls arrived back at Ellie's house and put away the food. Afterward, Ellie led April upstairs to a white room that looked like the others, except it had a little dresser and a bookshelf with a lamp on top.

"This'll be your room," said Ellie. April thanked Ellie and got herself arranged. As the day turned into night, Angelina sat in her bed.

She missed her friends.

She remembered all the good times she and her friends had back at the orphanage, how they were like her sisters because they were so close.

She remembered how much Ms. A was like a mother to her and how she had raised her ever since she was a baby. And Max, even if she had only known him for a few hours, she still missed him, and he was her friend.

"As soon as Magictopia is freed, then I can go back home."

CHAPTER ELEVEN
WINTERS' FOREST

THE NEXT DAY EARLY IN THE MORNING, the girls met up in Angelina's room and opened the origin book. They looked over the map and thought about where they should go next.

"We should go to Winters' Forest," said April. "It'd be best since we're looking for the element of ice."

"I've got just the thing for the trip, too!" announced Ellie. She hurried out of the room and came back with an arm full of coats. They were gold, pink, lavender, and light green. "I made these last night since the next element is ice. I figured that we would need these."

"Good thinking Ellie," said Angelina. "We're also going to have to pack some food. The forest is a long way from here compared to the other places."

***

THE DARK QUEEN was stomping back and forth. The sound was so loud you could hear the anger in her heels.

"I CAN'T BELIEVE THEY'VE GOTTEN A STEP AHEAD OF ME!" She stopped and snapped her fingers. The elf from the watchtower ran into the room.

"Roger, go get Eartha and Gage," the Dark Queen commanded.

"Yes, ma'am," said the elf. He ran into the training room, where Eartha and Gage were training. They were both in their late twenties. Eartha had a lean, toned figure, and she had dark green skin with long, dark green, curly hair. Her cruel, grim eyes were greenish-brown. She wore a long dress made out of giant leaves, with one long sleeve around her shoulder.

Gage was an ice elf; he was a tall, slim, sophisticated looking man with short dark brown hair that he kept neat. His eyes were white and looked like they could freeze you to death with one cold stare. He wore a long midnight blue suit with a long blue cape and black boots.

"Eartha, element of pollution and Gage element of dark ice," announced the elf. The two stopped their training and looked at the elf.

"You are assigned to kill the elements of creation." Eartha and Gage shared a grim smile.

"Finally, after all these years. A real battle," said Gage. The two of them flew out the window, beginning their quest to find the elements.

***

Back at the winter forest, the girls ventured through the snow and ice, the wind cold and bitter.

"It's getting colder," said April.

"And windy!" complained Ellie, getting the hair out of her eyes.

"It means we're getting close," said Angelina. Her necklace began to glow as it pulled her forward.

"This way, guys!" she called. Everyone followed her as her necklace took them further into the forest until it suddenly stopped. They looked around. There was nothing; no one was there, just ice and snow.

"What? That doesn't make any sense," said Opal.

"Why did the necklace take us here?" questioned April.

"Who's there?" asked a voice. The girls looked around to find who said that, yet they couldn't see with the wind blinding them. Then it stopped, making everything clear. There standing before them, was a young pixie.

Her skin was tan, her thin, long black hair flowing in the wind. She had pointed ears like an elf, except they were shorter in comparison. Her crystal white wings glistened softly.

The pixie wore surprisingly fewer clothes despite the blistering weather. She wore a grey turtleneck sweater and a dark blue skirt with black shoes.

Her thin icy blue eyes stared the girls down as if she was trying to freeze them just with her stare.

Angelina cleared her throat and began to speak.

"Um, hello. I'm Angelina, and these are my friends Ellie, Opal, and April." She gestured towards the elements.

"We came here in search of someone. I know this is going to sound crazy, but...I'm the lost princess." The pixie only scoffed in disbelief.

"The lost princess? Do you honestly expect me to believe in something so ridiculous? Wasn't the royal family murdered?"

"That would be correct," a sinister voice answered.

The girls turned around. There they saw Eartha and Gage in the air, looking down at them, like prey ready to be eaten.

"And soon, you'll end up just like them!" said Eartha with a cruel smile on her lips. Together, Eartha and Gage combined their dark magic, forming a huge, root-frost monster. The creature let out a terrifying roar, then slammed its giant hand at the girls.

The pixie from before ran, hiding behind a rock that was at a safe distance from the battle. The elements exchanged a look.

"Looks like it's time to transform!" said Angelina.

"Wait, how do you transform?" asked April.

"You say your name and what element you are," explained Ellie.

April nodded and took a deep breath.

"April, element of nature!"

April gasped as she found herself in the air. Greenlight from her earrings twirled her hair, giving her a long braid in the middle of her hair. The magic spun around her, transforming her plain dress into a light green dress made out of leaves, with a huge cherry blossom around her waist and matching heels. Light green eyeshadow and red-orange lipstick shined on her face along with a silver green wood staff in her hand, and she landed back on the ground.

The monster formed giant icy rocks and threw them at the elements. Angelina threw her shield, crumbling the boulders before they could hit the ground. The beast threw another rock at Ellie; Ellie took into the sky, shooting arrows at the creature. The monster roared, and it threw more rocks, this time at April and Opal. April whacked an incoming rock to pieces while Opal cracked another with her whip. Opal turned to April.

"I've got an idea. I'll climb up the monster, and you take its lower half."

"Are you sure about that?" asked April, unsure her plan would work.

"Trust me, I got this," assured Opal.

April gave her a smile and nodded. The two of them charged while the monster was distracted with Angelina and Ellie. Opal hopped on the monster's foot and climbed her way up.

The beast saw her and tried to slam her with its giant hands, but Opal quickly made it up to its shoulder. She smacked the creature in the face. The monster wobbled but kept its stance.

"It looks like it's getting too easy for you. Let's see you try this!" said Eartha. She stomped her foot, and the ground shook and rumbled. Cracks formed, and substantial, thick vines emerged, wrapping around the elements. "Let us go!" shouted Angelina.

"Oh, I don't think so," said Gage, with an evil smile. He and Eartha stood side by side, pointing their hands at the elements. The pixie hiding watched as it all happened. She didn't know whether she should do something or stay where she was. She continued watching as the monster was getting closer to the elements, ready to crush them.

I can't just stand here doing nothing, She thought. After a frustrating debate with herself, she took off into the air, shooting ice crystals at the monster, turning its attention to her. The beast roared and tried swatting the pixie like an annoying fly. But the pixie was fast, so fast she was nothing but a blur.

"What is that!?" asked Eartha.

"It's another brat to kill!" said Gage, filling with anger. The two of them blasted their dark magic at the pixie, yet she flew past their attacks, firing back at them.

The monster then joined in, throwing massive punches at her. The pixie turned and ducked past its hits and shot more crystals at Eartha and Gage, slicing Eartha's cheek and Gage's shoulder.

"Why, you little pest!" Eartha yelled, rage filling in her eyes. Vines emerged from the ground and grabbed the pixie. The pixie struggled to break free, but the vines had a tight grip on her. Gage and Eartha laughed as they watched her struggle. Gage took a step forward.

"Let's see how fast you are now!" mocked Gage. He aimed his hand at the pixie, dark magic forming, and he blasted it at her. The pixie gasped. Time seemed to slow down as the pixie was getting closer to her fate. She put up her hand, trying to block the hit, knowing it was useless yet still hoping something would happen.

A sapphire ring then appeared on her finger, stopping Gage's attack.

Everyone gasped at what had just happened, especially the pixie who muttered in shock.

"W-what? What's happening!?"

"...Wait...I get it now!" said Ellie.

"What do you mean?" asked Angelina.

"Remember when my bracelet appeared?"

"Yeah."

"That's because the jewelry appears when someone is chosen!"

"Oh, ...it all makes sense now!" said Angelina.

Before she could understand what just happened, the pixie's ring shined, freeing her from the vines and beginning her transformation. Light combed through her hair, giving her an icy blue hairpin in the shape of a snowflake. Her sweater and skirt changed into an icy blue shimmering flowing dress, completed with matching gloves and ice crystal heels. The magic finished her off by giving her frosty blue eyeshadow and red-violet lipstick.

When she was lowered back to the ground, the pixie gazed at herself in amazement.

"I... can't believe it," she said softly. Her daydreaming was cut short by the sound of slow clapping.

"Wasn't that a nice little show you put on," said Gage.

"But I think it's time we get back to the battle and finish you off!" Eartha shot vines at the pixie. She flew around, avoiding them, and cut the rest of the elements free from the cage.

"Thank you," said Angelina.

"Sun-he," said the pixie. "My name is Sun-he."

"Thank you, Sun-he," said Angelina with a smile. Gage began blasting giant icicles at them. Angelina blocked them with her shield. The monster let out a huge gust of wind, nearly knocking down the elements.

"I have an idea," said Sun-he.

"What is it?" asked Angelina.

"The rest of you distract it. I need you to help me," she said, pointing to April. Opal, Ellie, and Angelina attacked the monster with all they had. Ellie shot her arrows, Angelina blasted beams of light, and Opal smacked it with her whip. Sun-he and April were off to the side; the pixie used all her energy and formed a giant ice ball.

"Alright, I need you to hit this at the monster," Sun-he ordered.

"Are you sure?" April asked doubtingly. "I don't know if I'm that strong."

"I'm sure," Sun-he said with a confident smile. April took a deep breath and nodded.

"On the count of three. One… two… three!" yelled Sun-he. She threw the ball towards April. April focused and, using all her might, hit the ball straight at the monster. The ball hit the monster directly in the head, and the beast fell to the ground with a great crash, not getting up. The girls took a moment to regain their energy.

"I have to admit. We didn't think you'd make it this far. But now it's time we finish what we came for," Eartha said, smiling grimly.

She and Gage stood side by side, their hands next to each other. Their powers combined, forming a massive orb of dark magic. The elements watched as the orb got bigger and bigger.

Once it was big enough, Eartha and Gage launched it at them. The ball came crashing down at the elements.

Angelina ran up in front of the others, pulling out a shield and blocking it. Angelina used all her might pushing back the orb, but she wasn't as strong, and she could feel herself being pushed back by the force. She closed her eyes as she resisted giving up.

Suddenly it felt like she was stronger and was able to drive back the orb harder. When she opened her eyes, she found the rest of the elements shoving with her.

She smiled, refocusing her energy, and joined the others. Together they pushed the orb back at Gage and Eartha, blasting them out of sight.

The girls fell to the ground, finally being able to relax.

"That was amazing!" Opal said.

"Yeah, I'd have to say that was our best moment so far," agreed Ellie. Angelina turned to Sun-he.

"So, do you believe us now?" she asked, jokingly.

"Well, it would be foolish not to," said Sun-he smiling at Angelina. The two shook hands.

"Welcome to the team," Angelina said proudly.

"Yay! Our team is almost complete. Now, all we need is the element of fire!" Opal cheered.

"I know just the person," said Sun-he. "But it's going to be a long journey, and it's already sunset. So I suggest you spend the night at my home and then we'll go in the morning."

She led them to her house, where they rested for their journey to The Fire Grounds.

CHAPTER TWELVE
THE FIRE GROUNDS

THE DARK QUEEN was sitting still on the throne. She gave a grim still face, then stood up and yelled.

"I CAN'T BELIEVE THEY'RE THIS CLOSE TO FINDING THE LAST ELEMENT!" she yelled.

"We apologize, our darkness," said Eartha and Gage.

"How is it they keep winning?" asked the Dark Queen.

Gage spoke.

"Well, my queen. It appears they've been getting strong-"

"SILENCE!" the queen hushed, glaring at Gage.

"Leave; you are no use to me now," she ordered.

Gage and Eartha left the room. The Dark Queen summoned an elf servant.

"Roger, go get Rick," she ordered.

"My queen, what about Angela?" asked the elf. "Did you want me to get her too?" "I'll handle her," said The Dark Queen.

The elf nodded and walked off. He then entered a hot room that had giant holes in the ground with hot water shooting out of them.

In the middle of the room, a man leaned against a giant rock, sound asleep. He had slim, a toned build to him, his skin dark, and his eyes were covered with black sunglasses. He wore a black leather jacket with flames painted on its back, and his hair was styled in a faux hawk fading yellow to red.

"Rick, element of dark flame, or should we call you Ricky?" the elf summoned.

"Huh?" Rick woke up, standing to his feet.

"You and Angela are assigned to destroy the elements of creation before they find the last element," said the elf.

"It doesn't matter what you call me," Rick grinned.

"Finally, it's the fire master's turn," he boasted as he flipped his collar.

The Dark Queen walked up to Angela's room door, opening it and walking into the room.

"Angela, I need to discuss something with you," she said with her fake loving voice and concerned eyes.

"Mother, what's going on?" asked Angela.

"It appears that we've entered a war with thieves who are trying to take over the kingdom," the Dark Queen explained.

"What!?" gasped Angela.

"I'm afraid so dear, and it looks like they're winning so far. So close, they can overthrow us."

Angela's face was a mixture of anger and shock.

"How is this happening?" she asked, nearly out of anger.

"I'm sorry I didn't tell you sooner, but I thought we'd defeat them by now," said the queen, stroking Angela's cheek. Angela looked down, rage filling inside her. How dare someone try to steal their kingdom and home. The Dark Queen lifted Angela's head so that she was staring down at Angela's dark honey brown eyes while Angela gazed at her dark blue pools.

"But that's why I came here. I had hope that you and Rick could take down those monsters and stop this once and for all." Her voice lingered a hint of her regular sinisterness as she said that.

"Do you have what it takes?"

"Yes," Angela responded with determination. The Dark Queen let go of her face and smiled at her. They left the room and met up in the throne room where Rick waited.

"Now go and make me proud," the queen said, looking at Angela.

"Don't worry, mother. I won't let you down!" Angela promised. With that, she and Rick flew off, starting their mission to find the elements of creation.

"That's my girl," the Dark Queen said in satisfaction.

***

THE GIRLS TRAVELED through the Fire Grounds, following behind Sun-he.

"It's getting hotter," said Angelina tying her coat around her waist.

"We're getting close; Suez comes here to practice," assured Sun-he.

"The grounds here are surprisingly well grown," said April, looking at the few growing plants.

"Here should be good," said Sun-he. They stopped and looked around.

"Is anyone here?" called Angelina.

"Who's there!?" demanded a voice from behind the trees.

"There's no need to fight; we come in peace," assured Angelina.

"Who's there!?" demanded the voice again.

"Suez! It's me," Sun-he called.

Silence stood for a second before a fire elf came out from behind the trees.

The elf had a slightly toned build with broad wide shoulders. Her messy white-blonde hair was cut in a pixie bobbed style. She wore a black crop top with baggy cargo pants held up with a belt decorated with chains and high plated black sneakers. Her fierce brown eyes were like sharp knives piercing into the girls' very souls. She turned to Sun-he.

"After all these years. You got some nerve crawling back here with your little friends." She cast the rest of the elements with an annoyed side glance. Sun-he fumed with anger; she was about to fire back a snarky remark, but Angelina spoke up before she could.

"Look, I understand you two aren't on the best terms with each other, but we're on an important mission, and we need you."

Suez gave Angelina the same death stare she gave Sun-he.

"You expect me to go anywhere with her?" she asked, pointing at Sun-he.

"Look, Suez, I know we had our differences in the past, but right now is very important," Sun-he explained.

"Forget it. I'd rather die than do anything with her around!" Suez stormed off. Angelina and Sun-he hurried after her.

"Please! We need you. You're our last hope!" begged Angelina.

"No! I can't stand her!" said Suez.

Angelina stopped and turned to Sun-he.

"What happened between you two to make her hate you so much?"

"Suez and I were once friends, but then one day, we got into a fight, and we became enemies. I'm surprised she didn't hit me as soon as she saw me!" explained Sun-he.

"Well, isn't there some way for you guys to make up?" asked Angelina.

Sun-he shook her head.

"It's no use; she and I hate each other. This is the first time I've since her in seven years."

"Well, we have to think of something. Without her, the elements of creation aren't complete," said Angelina.

"Well, well, lookie what we have here," a deep voice called from behind. The elements turned around to see Rick and Angela in the air staring down at them. Rick had an evil grin on his face while Angela only stared at them with a straight, disgusted look.

"You must be the elements of creation," commented Rick. "Weird, I'd thought you would look more of a threat. Oh, well, that just makes this job easier!" They fused their powers, forming a giant, sinister dark flame monster. It was even more significant than the last monster, and it was no doubt even more powerful.

The elements transformed and pulled out their weapons, but as Angelina turned to Angela, she was overwhelmed with shock and confusion. The girl looked just like her, how...why? Was this some trick from the Dark Queen to throw her off?

Her train of thought was cut off when the monster shaped a colossal fireball and fired it like a baseball.

The girls leaped past the spinning ball. Angelina crafted a beam of golden light and lunged at the flaming beast.

The monster responded to her attack by sending powerful waves of fire. Angelina's shield covered her from the hissing flames.

The monster fired its dark energy at Ellie and April. Ellie fired an arrow, destroying the attack.

The giant flower around April's dress glowed as she crafted thorns as big as swords. April aimed them at the monster, then fired them like missiles. The beast only swatted her attack with a wave of its massive hand.

"You know, I feel like we're missing out on all the fun. So why don't we hop in," Rick said, looking at Angela with an evil grin. They added to the monster punches and strikes by blasting dark beams at the elements. The elements struggled to fend off the sudden attacks while trying to get in a hit. Sun-he was able to somewhat keep up with the battle's frantic atmosphere, missing Angela's clash by a second and blasting an ice crystal at Rick. The crystal nicked his hand, making it bleed. Rick looked around to see who the culprit was. He spotted Sun-he glaring at him and gave her a cold stare.

"You made the wrong choice, snowflake!" He threw her large balls of fire, Sun-he blocked his shots with her halberd. Ricky hit her again. This time Sun-he was unable to avoid the hit fast enough, causing her to crash to the ground. She tried to get up, but Ricky's attack left her weak, and her arm was badly burned and blistered. Ricky hovered over her with a sickening grin on his face.

"Not so cool now, are you snowflake?" He was about to finish her off for good when Suez came running, pushing Sun-he out of the way before Rick could kill her off.

"Y… you saved me..." said Sun-he, shocked.

"Even if I said I hate you, I couldn't just stand there and watch you die," Suez said with a grin.

A fire-red watch flashed on her wrist, and she was lifted into the air.

"Hey! What is going on here!?" demanded Suez.

Red magic swapped her clothes with a fiery red tank top, and shorts, and boots. It whipped through her hair, leaving red highlights. When she returned to the ground, she looked at her new outfit and felt the magic through her veins.

"W-what is this?" she asked, trying to grab hold of what just happened.

"Suez, you're the element of fire," Sun-he explained.

"I am?" Suez gasped, looking at her new outfit. She turned to the monster, feeling the power in her blood rush, and charged at the creature, giving it a powerful punch to the leg. The beast wobbled, nearly collapsing to the ground. She ran up to the beast again, giving it another great hit.

"Looks like I'm getting the hang of this," Suez said with a proud and smug look.

"It seems that they've found the element of fire," Angela noted.

"In that case, it's time we finish them off!" Angela and Rick charged the monster up with more dark power, making it bigger and more powerful.

Together, Rick, Angela, and the beast blasted out energy at the elements.

Angelina created a bubble to protect them.

I've got it! Thought Suez. She got out of the bubble, jumped high in the air, and gave the monster a mega punch. It dissolved in the flames while Angela and Rick were blasted off. Suez landed to the ground, and the rest of the elements came over.

"Are you guys okay!?" asked Ellie.

They all looked at Suez.

"So, Suez, does this mean you're joining the elements of creation, even if Sun-he is here?"

"I'll admit it's gonna take some time for me to get used to her," Suez began. "But, I wouldn't give this up for nothing." She flashed a smile. Angelina smiled as the two of them shook hands, and the rest of the elements celebrated.

"Finally, our team is complete!" cheered Opal.

***

BY THE TIME THEY ARRIVED at Ellie's house, night had fallen. Ellie showed Suez to her new room. It was a light red colored room that looked like the other rooms, except it had a rug in the middle of the floor.

Ellie had noticed how each room matched the elements. When she decorated them, it was a mere choice of style, yet she wondered if it was beyond that.

Suez got herself arranged, and soon, the day melted into sunset. Angelina looked out her window gazing at the golden sun fading into a mix of pink, yellow, purple, and blue. Excitement filled her heart as she thought about the future of the elements now that they were complete. Yet her heart sank a little at the thought of them eventually having to face the Dark Queen. She knew it would happen, yet she never put any thinking into it until now, which made her scared.

The Dark Queen was powerful, and she feared that they wouldn't be strong enough to defeat her. Her thoughts took a grim turn as she pictured what would happen if things did go that way. She closed her eyes, stopping those thoughts, and reassured herself.

Everything will be fine. It's gonna be hard, but we'll be able to do it. She took a deep breath before opening her eyes again. Laying down in her bed, she reassured herself once more before closing her eyes and going to sleep.

CHAPTER THIRTEEN
TRAINING DAY

Angelina woke up early in the morning. This time, it wasn't the warm light of the golden sun that woke her but the sound of grunting and fighting from outside.

She rubbed the tiredness out of her eyes, got dressed, and headed outside to see what was making the noise. When she walked out, she was surprised to see Sun-he transformed, practicing her fighting skills with her halberd in hand.

"I didn't think you would be out here this early," Angelina said. Sun-he stopped her fighting, turned around, and smiled at Angelina.

"I thought I'd go and start getting the hang of my powers," replied Sun-he.

"Sounds fun. Can I join?" Angelina asked.

"Of course, we can try going head to head," suggested Sun-he.

Angelina pulled out her shield; the two of them shared a ready look and charged at each other.

Sun-he clashed her halberd, Angelina blocked her with her shield, along with blasting her with a golden beam. Sun-he repelled the beam with her weapon, striking shards of ice.

Angelina blocked with her shield again, this time throwing it and shooting more beams. Sun-he was too slow to respond, knocking her to the ground.

"You okay?" asked Angelina.

"Yes, that wasn't too bad for a first time," said Sun-he, getting up. The rest of the elements appeared, walking up to the two.

"What's with all the noise?" asked Ellie.

"We're training. Want to join?" asked Angelina.

"You bet! It's you versus me, pixie dust!" said Suez pulling out her gauntlets.

"Careful Suez, don't let the fire get to your head," teased Sun-he.

"Come on, April, you and I can go toe to toe," said Opal, pulling April.

April interjected.

"I don't know if I-" Opal grabbed her before she could finish; she shrugged and followed. Suez and Sun-he went up face-to-face with their weapons.

"Ready pixie dust?" joked Suez.

"Only if you are, hot head," replied Sun-he. She clashed her weapon. Suez grabbed it and pushed it back.

"Not bad," said Sun-he.

"Not too bad yourself," said Suez with a grin. She blasted a bolt of fire. Sun-he whacked it back at her, lunging her halberd at Suez, who caught it in her hands.

She used all her strength and concentration, and her gauntlets had lit on fire. Sun-he tried her best as Suez was slowly pushing her back. She closed her eyes and only focused on ice. With all her might, her halberd froze Suez in place. Sun-he aimed her halberd at Suez with a smile; Suez shared the smile.

"Impressive." Angelina was in mid-battle with Ellie. Ellie shot an arrow, Angelina smacked it away with her shield. Ellie darted more shafts; Angelina shot back a beam of light. The two attacks out powered each other, resulting in a blast that knocked both girls down. When they got up, they shared a smile.

"Nice job," complemented Angelina.

"Same to you," said Ellie.

"Ready, April?" asked. Opal.

April was a little unsure yet nodded anyway. Opal charged at her with her whip, jumping into the air and coming back down, ready to hit. April pointed her staff at her, with long, robust vines shooting from it and wrapping tightly around Opal. With her one free hand still holding her whip, Opal smacked April's hand, setting herself free.

Throughout the day, the elements trained, getting the hang of their weapons, and practicing their new powers.

Soon it was sundown.

The girls had retreated back inside, refreshing themselves. Ellie came in with a tray of tasty popsicles.

"Anyone want a frozen treat?" she offered. The elements grabbed one and enjoyed their refreshing treat after a long hard day.

"These are better than my ma's hot fudge rock pops," said Suez.

"Just what I needed, too," commented April. They then began discussing when they should train again, agreeing to do it every day to master their powers. The conversation then turned more relaxed with them, the girls laughing and joking with each other as they ate their frozen treats. Soon early night began to fall, and an idea popped into Angelina's mind.

"Hey, we should have a slumber party!" she suggested. The only reaction she got was puzzled expressions from her friends.

"What's a 'slumber party'?" asked Ellie.

"It's something we do on Earth for fun. They take place at night, you invite all your friends to your house, and you stay up doing fun activities," said Angelina. The elements agreed.

"That sounds fun!" Opal said excitedly.

"Yeah, why not," agreed Suez.

They made snacks and held the slumber party in Ellie's room. The girls gossiped, laughed, and did all kinds of fun things they could think of for the whole night. Ellie decided to sew pajamas for everyone for the special occasion.

"And finished!" announced Ellie. Each pair was made with wool and in the same color as their element. The girls tried them on and looked in the mirror.

"What do you think?" asked Ellie excitedly, waiting for their response.

"They're great, Ellie," said Angelina, looking in the mirror.

"They're so soft too," added Opal.

"Thanks, Ellie," said Sun-he.

"Where'd you learn to make clothes?" asked Suez.

"My family owns a tailor shop, so naturally, I was taught sewing," answered Ellie. "I always wanted to inherit it and make it into one of the most successful shops in all of Magictopia. Where people far and wide, even the wealthiest, would come and admire my work.

"I bet it would be just that great," said April.

"You know, that mention of family reminds me of mine," spoke Suez. "I've got six brothers, and I'm the only girl.

"*Six* brothers?" asked a shocked Opal.

"How did you survive that?" asked Angelina.

"It wasn't so bad. We were all raised to be tough, and I never felt like an outcast, especially since I'm the strongest out of all of them. You know I took them all down...at once. So it's safe to say I earned that spot."

"Well, that sure explains your fiery attitude," commented Ellie.

"You know, I sometimes miss my home. I miss swimming in the water and going exploring and seeing the variety of creatures that lived there. Sometimes when I have a chance to myself, I would use them as a reference for my art or wait until sunset to capture its beauty," said Opal.

"I know how you feel. I've never been outside my homeland, and I already miss the crisp cold air," Sun-he spoke. "When I was younger, my mother would take my sister and me to a frozen lake, and we would skate there and pretend as if we were dancing on the ice."

"I remember that lake. We'd used to go there all the time," added Suez.

"Wow, you all sound like you had exciting and interesting lives," joined April. "I had a pretty ordinary home life. I was an only child and a shy person, so I didn't have that many friends. Well...any people friends. Animals connected with me. I felt like myself around them as to actual people. Maybe that's why I was chosen to be the element of nature."

***

SOON IT WAS TIME TO SLEEP. Everyone slept in extra blankets and pillows on the floor.

Angelina was happy today had happened. Not only did she improve in her magic, but she also felt that everyone was getting closer, almost becoming friends. It made her have hope that they would be able to defeat the Dark Queen once and for all. She cleared her mind before resting her eyes and going to sleep.

CHAPTER FOURTEEN
EARTH

BACK ON EARTH, chaos took control at the orphanage. Ms. A called the police, who started a search for Angelina. They put up missing posters and questioned everyone who talked to Angelina last, who were Leona, Avery, Sophia, Violet, Ms. A., and Max. In Rainbow Waters, chatter and rumors about Angelina spread like wildfire. People gossiped about what happened before Angelina ran away, about her necklace. Those who witnessed the incident told their friends what happened, fabricating it to make it sound more interesting. Some said that Angelina was a witch, while others believed she was part of a cult; others chose not to believe in either. The gossip only grew when Violet claimed that Angelina was a terrible person who tried to hurt her because she was jealous of Violet— leading more hate to come to Angelina as well.

Sophia opened her locker, and she took out a picture with Angelina and the rest of her friends together. She sighed as she thought about Angelina. Where was she? Was she safe? What could have happened to her?

"Hey," said Leona softly as she and Avery walked up to Sophia.

"Hey," replied Sophia sadly.

They didn't say anything else to each other and avoided eye contact. Ever since Angelina left, they drifted apart. They were too overcome with fear of what happened to their friend and little sister. Things just weren't the same without her; she was the missing piece of the puzzle. And now, with her gone, their friendship was taking a rocky turn.

"It's just not the same without Angelina," said Avery, breaking the silence.

"I know, I can't stop thinking about what could happen to her," said Sophia. They stopped their conversation when they heard chatter in the halls.

"Did you hear about the girl who went missing?" asked one guy. "I heard she's part of a cult," said another guy.

"She might as well be a witch. Violet told me that she threatened her. And that's why she left," another girl commented.

"What a freak. Can't believe she was at our school."

"I'm just glad she's gone, hope she stays like that," began another girl.

"Yeah, I hope she stays missing for good. Who knows what she could've done."

"Hey!" yelled Leona, all eyes on her. Leona felt rage boil over her.

"What is wrong with you all? Someone who you don't even know is gone, and all you can do is say horrible things about her?"

"Leona's right. You people just love to gossip about others without knowing the story or their character," protested Sophia.

"Guys, please don't start any trouble," begged Avery, holding her friend's arms to stop them from doing anything crazy.

"What's going on here?" asked Violet, joining the conversation. "You three standing up for a freak like her? Why am I not surprised?" She said with a bitter smile.

"Angelina is not a freak. Even she didn't know what happened. She was just confused just as you!" protested Avery.

"Are you honestly standing up for someone like her? Someone who threatens another person. For all we know, she could be a witch in disguise, plotting on her next victim!" said Violet grimly.

"That's enough, Violet," Max said, walking up to Violet. "There's no need to talk about Angelina like that."

"I'm just telling the truth," said Violet. "That your dear Angelina is nothing but a she-devil, who should be dead if she isn't already."

"How could you even say that!?" demanded Avery.

"You always act like you're the queen who can treat everyone like trash, expecting people to wait on you hand and foot," said Leona.

"Yeah! You think you're so great and amazing when you're just like everyone else!" joined Sophia.

"You say Angelina's a monster, but that's not true. You're the monster!"

Everyone gasped. No one had ever said that to Violet, especially to her face. Violet just stood there, her jaw wide open. How could someone say anything like that to her? Her family was one of the richest in New York, and she was the most popular girl at school. Everyone worshiped her. Yet someone had the nerve to call Violet Crystal a monster.

"Okay! Shows over, everyone get to class!" ordered a teacher, coming into the hall. Everyone went to their classes as they chattered about Sophia calling Violet, the school's queen, a monster. Violet just stood there, trying to understand what happened.

"Miss Violet, what are you waiting for?" asked the teacher. Violet growled, flipped her hair, and stormed off to class.

***

Meanwhile, back at Magictopia, Angela was in the training room.

She was trying to practice her spells, but her mind was flooded with a variety of thoughts.

Why do those people want to take the kingdom? How can they be that powerful? How am I going to beat them? She thought as she paced back and forth.

"I see you have a lot on your mind," said Rebecca, coming into the room. Angela turned around to see Rebecca.

"Oh, Rebecca," she said softly. "I was just practicing for the next battle."

"So am I," said Rebecca. She noticed the sad look on Angela's face. "What's wrong?" she asked.

"Nothing, just...tired," lied Angela.

"There must be something," said Rebecca. Her tone was softer and kinder than it usually was. Angela sighed. Rebecca had always been like an older sister to her; she felt more comfortable talking to her than the other elements.

"I'm just so scared that I won't be strong enough to defeat those trying to steal the kingdom. I feel if I fail to protect my kingdom, then I'll let everyone down...even mother." Angela put her head down so Rebecca couldn't see the tears in her eyes.

"I know how you feel." Angela's eyes widened with shock. Rebecca never admitted she felt weak.

"Y...you do?"

"I know how it feels, not wanting to let down the ones you care about," said Rebecca. "Especially when they're all you have," the words came out as a desperate whisper.

"What was that?" asked Angela, barely hearing what she said.

"Nothing, nothing," stuttered Rebecca. "But, I know what you're going through, and I can help. I can help you train for the next battle."

"You will?" asked Angela.

"Yes," said Rebecca.

"Thank you, Rebecca," said Angela; she felt warm knowing that Rebecca was willing to take the time to help her. This happened before; it was like Rebecca's way of showing she cared about her.

"Let's get started then. We don't want to waste any time," said Rebecca.

"Right," replied Angela. They began their training. Rebecca taught Angela how to improve her attacks and defenses while she herself improved.

CHAPTER FIFTEEN
MS. A

MS. A SAT IN THE KITCHEN, a cup of tea in her hand. She had been under a lot of stress and emotions since Angelina's disappearance. The police hadn't updated her on the case; the last time she had spoken to them was when they interviewed her. Ms. A still had hope in her heart; Angelina was out there. She answered every call she received in the chance someone might know where Angelina was. But none of them helped. Ms. A took a sip of her tea as she gazed at a photo of Angelina in front of her.

"I know you're out there. If you are, please come home. Everything feels so strange without you here. The girls miss you like crazy. Leona, Avery, and Sophia have drifted apart since you left. I can't even sleep knowing you're gone..."

The woman stopped once she realized she was talking to a photo and turned away.

"Great, now I'm going crazy," she sighed. She put her hands on her face as she felt a sob in her throat.

"I wish someone could just tell me you're okay."

Suddenly her phone began to ring. Ms. A's eyes brightened with hope.

"Please, be about Angelina," she said with desperation.

She quickly picked up the phone and answered the random number.

"Hello?" Ms. A said.

"Hello," answered a woman. "Is this Miss Anderson?"

"This is her," said Ms. A. "Who is this?"

"My name is Jerrica Golden, and I saw the news about Angelina." Ms. A felt the sound of her heart pounding ring in her ears.

"Do you know where she is?" she asked, trying not to give away the desperation and excitement in her voice.

"I wish I did, but unfortunately, that is not why I called," said the woman. The disappointment felt like a stab in Ms. A's heart. She wanted to just hang up on the woman for wasting her time.

"Look, I don't know who you are, so if you're going to waste my ti-"

"Please don't hang up. This is important," pleaded the woman.

Ms. A stopped. There had to be a reason why this random woman called her, especially if it involved Angelina. She sighed and spoke to the woman again.

"I'm listening." She heard the woman let out a breath of relief before she explained herself.

"I know this is going to sound strange, but...I believe I'm Angelina's aunt." Ms. A nearly jumped out of her seat when she heard the news. Angelina had an aunt? How? When? Angelina never had any family members, yet this woman had claimed to be her aunt.

"H-hold, on. How is that possible?"

"I was just as shocked as you when I found out myself,

"You see, fourteen years ago, my brother and his wife died. I figured that my nieces had passed as well until last week when I saw Angelina's picture on the news. She looks so similar to my niece. That's why I thought she was." Ms. A ran her fingers through her hair. First, Angelina disappears, and now a woman claims to be her aunt? How was she even sure this woman was telling the truth? She could be lying for all she knew. Yet, there was something deep within Ms. A's heart that told her the woman was telling the truth. After all, she called in the hopes of finding the niece she thought had died.

"I know this all may be a bit overwhelming, especially with these recent events. But I just wanted to give you my address in case Angelina returns," said Jerrica.

"Of course, what is your address?" asked Ms. A, taking out a pen and a sticky note.

"It's 1493 Hoffman Avenue," said Jerrica.

"Alright, I got it down," said Ms. A

"Great, and thank you. Please keep me updated on Angelina if the police tell you anything," Jerrica pleaded.

"Of course, and you're welcome," said Ms. A.

She hung up the phone and looked at the address. She let out an exhausted sigh.

"First Angelina goes missing, now this." She said as she rubbed her face.

"I'm going to need more tea," she remarked before fixing herself another cup.

CHAPTER SIXTEEN
NIGHTMARE

ANGELINA FOUND HERSELF in the orphanage; it was dark and empty. There seemed to be no one in there. The mysterious atmosphere sent a chill down her back.

"Hello, Ms. A?" Angelina called. No answer. "Leona? Sophia? Avery?" Still no answer. *Why is no one here?* She thought. She debated on her next plan of action when she saw something in the corner of her eye. She turned to see a golden light glowing from upstairs. She wondered whether or not she should follow it. Feeling as if she should follow it, she walked up the stairs and walked through the hall. She stopped when she found the light coming from inside her old room; the door was half-open. Gaining her courage, she slowly opened the door and peeked inside. The light was sitting on her desk, and it stood there as if it was waiting for Angelina. Angelina carefully walked up to it and gazed at it.

Suddenly the light glowed, filling the room with its golden shine and blinding her. The light then dimmed. Angelina opened her eyes to see the illusion of a man and a woman.

The woman was beautiful; her black hair was like long curls of silk trailing to her feet. Her skin was as smooth as chocolate. Her massive angel wings seemed so soft and beautiful as they sparkled under the light. She had the same eyes as Angelina, except hers were like shimmering blue diamonds.

A gold crown decorated with gems was placed on her head, with a white flowing dress embellished with gold embroidery. Next to her was a handsome, bold looking man with a strong fit build and a mocha tone. His black hair was braided in dreadlocks, and he wore a gold crown just like the woman. His eyes were black brown and were filled with kindness. He wore a white suit, along with a golden cape and knee-high boots. Angelina gazed at the two. For some reason, she felt she had known them before, even though she hadn't seen them before. They both gave her the feeling of safety, love, and warmth, making Angelina feel comfortable.

"Hello, Angelina," the woman finally spoke. Her voice was so calm and soothing, much like Ms. A's.

"You know who I am?" Angelina asked. How did this woman know her name when she didn't know who she was.

"Because we know who you are," the woman spoke again.

"We're your parents." Angelina's eyes widened as the words sank in.

"Y… y… you are?" the young girl said, tears filling in her eyes.

"Yes," the woman said with a smile. Her parents were right in front of her; she had waited for this day for so long. They were better than any fantasy she could dream of. They were perfect. The woman reached out her hand as if offering Angelina to join them. Without hesitation or wondering whether or not it was real, Angelina got ready to touch the woman's hand.

"Mama," she said softly.

The golden light from before vanished, and the room was filled with cold, bitter darkness. Angelina froze, looking around the now changed room. She watched in horror as her parents' skin melted, turning them into skeletons, and their bones fell to the floor. The bones shriveled into ash. The ashes lifted into the air, spinning and spinning until the Dark Queen appeared in their place. The Dark Queen laughed maniacally as Angelina gasped in fear. The Dark Queen composed herself and gazed at Angelina.

"Well, now, what do we have here? After all these years, we meet again." A wicked smile curved on her lips. Angelina glared at the queen with a mixture of shock, sadness, and anger, tears still in her eyes.

"I have to admit it was quite interesting. Watching you think that your parents had come back, only to find that they're still dead."

"Y...you monster! Trapping me in one of your little games!" Angelina yelled sharply.

"When I defeat you, I'll make sure you feel the same pain I went through!" The Dark Queen laughed again.

"Do you honestly think you can defeat me? Your own mother couldn't, and she was in full control of her powers. And you?" The queen stepped closer to Angelina, making Angelina step back until she was cornered into the wall.

"You're nothing but a weak, pathetic mistake that will never defeat me. Even if you hide, I'll find you." She put her face up to her and said in a low voice. "The more you hide, I'll keep attacking."

With that, she lunged at Angelina.

Angelina woke up on the floor from Ellie's sleepover. Sweat dripped from her forehead, and she was in complete tears.

"It... was... just... a dream," she stuttered. Angelina took in deep breaths, trying to calm herself and not wake the others. She sat there, with the Dark Queen's haunting words repeating in her mind. *The more you hide, I'll keep attacking.*

***

THE NEXT MORNING, the elements of destruction and the Dark Queen were in the throne room, discussing what they had planned for the elements of creation.

"It appears phase one of the plan has worked, and now it's time to unleash phase two." The Dark Queen said.

"You know what to do, right?" she asked, looking up at the dark elements.

"Yes, my queen, this time, there's no doubt we'll finish them off for good," assured Rebecca.

"Excellent," the Dark Queen said with a satisfied smile. She watched the dark elements fly off to set their plan in motion.

***

BACK AT ELLIE'S HOUSE, the girls were eating the vegetable and fruit breakfast April had cooked. Angelina barely ate anything due to her nightmare. She looked a wreck; she had dark bags under her eyes, her bright eyes dimmed to a dull shade, and her hair was an untamed mess.

"Angelina, are you okay?" asked Ellie, concerned.

"Yeah, you don't look so good," said Suez.

"Who me?" asked Angelina, slightly startled.

"Yes, you look like you haven't slept in days," said Sun-he.

"And you've barely eaten anything," April joined in.

"Oh, I'm fine, just a little tired. I had a bad dream last night," Angelina said, hoping no one would go deeper into it.

"Did you want to talk about it? Maybe it'll help," suggested April.

"No! I mean...no thanks, I don't wanna talk about it," Angelina responded. The girls nodded, continuing on with their breakfast.

CRASH!

Everyone stood, alert on their feet.

"What was that?" asked Opal.

"Whatever it was, it doesn't sound good," said Ellie.

They ran out the back to see the elements of destruction, destroying Ellie's small garden.

"Hey! I just planted those!" yelled Ellie.

"Well, well, well, if it isn't the elements of creation, in their PJs!?" laughed Rick. He and the dark elements laughed.

"That's enough out of you!" said Angelina. The elements transformed and pulled out their weapons.

"But, before we begin the battle, how was your dream, oh princess of light? I hope you know that it was a little gift from all of us," said Gage.

"Wait... YOU gave me that dream!?" shouted Angelina.

"Of course, it was the Dark Queen's plan herself. Just a little something and I can tell by the look on your face you enjoyed it!" Rebecca remarked. She smiled when she saw Angelina's face twisted with rage.

"I wouldn't keep talking if I were you. Stalling won't save you!" Suez shot a glare at Rebecca.

"Then let the battle begin," Eartha said.

The elements of creation were ready to attack when Angelina stopped them.

"Guys, stop." Her voice was stiff and cold.

"Angelina, what's wrong?" asked Ellie.

"I have a score to settle, and I don't want you to get involved," Angelina answered, her fists tightening. Before they could object, Angelina sealed her friends in a giant golden bubble.

"Angelina!" The girls yelled, banging on the bubble. Angelina ignored them and transformed, this time pulling out two golden shields.

"Isn't this interesting? You think you can defeat all of us on your own?" Rebecca said, amused. "

"You just made this easier than it was."

"Stop talking already!" Angelina yelled. She threw one of her shields at Rebecca.

Rebecca shot her grin before firing back a dark beam at her.

Angelina protected herself with her shield and blasted golden rays at the elements of destruction. The dark elements fought back with their own dark beams; their hits were more powerful than Angelina had predicted. She struggled to avoid them while she fired. When she lowered her guard for a second, Rick formed a fireball and launched it at her. Angelina was too slow to react.

The flames pushed her back hard, causing her to fall to the ground.

"Angelina!" her friends yelled in concern. Angelina sat up. She attempted to get up, but she was too weak to stand. The hit had made her nose bleed and scraped the left side of her body badly.

"Angelina, let us out. You can't fight alone!" Opal pleaded.

"Please, Angelina, let us out," added Suez.

"What a wonderful sight," Gage said, with his usual grim smile. "The Lost Princess that everyone had faith in and dreamed of is on the verge of her end.

At least now you'll finally get to be with your parents as you wanted!"

The words hit Angelina hard, and the memories from her nightmare came back. How dare they toy with her like that, make her fall into their little trap. After all the pain she had dealt with being an orphan, having to know that her parents were never coming back. Having thought she met them, only for it to be some sick game, to these monsters.

How. Dare. They. Angelina could feel the rage boiling over her again, her necklace glowing rapidly, giving her the strength to stand on her feet. The elements of destruction blasted all their magic in one, creating a dark rainbow of magic.

Angelina pushed the magic back with her shield, her body being slightly shoved away by the power. She focused her might and let out all her rage into her magic, forming a vast streak of golden light that she blasted at the elements of destruction.

The light launched them into the sky, in the direction of the Dark Queen's castle.

Angelina watched them fly away, taking deep breaths. She stopped, trembling before collapsing to the ground, crying her eyes out.

The bubble that had trapped the other elements disappeared, and they ran to Angelina, comforting her.

"Oh Angelina, we're glad you're okay," Ellie was the first to say, hugging Angelina.

"Can't believe what happened. I thought for a second you were gonna be done for," Suez commented.

"Please don't do that again. Things could've been worse," Sun-he lightly scolded.

"I'm...I'm...sorry guys," Angelina said through sobs.

"It's just that...I had this dream where I got to see my parents...but then the Dark Queen came.

"I just got so mad. They were toying with me. Using my weakness against me to try to put me in their sick game."

"We know how you feel," said Ellie. "We all had faced pain and misfortune from the Dark Queen. You're feeling it too. We've all faced new challenges with having to go up against something like this. When you don't know what to do, and it feels like everything is moving so fast, to where you don't know if you can handle it."

"Thanks, guys," Angelina said, smiling softly. Her smile faded. "But I can't help thinking we need to defeat the Dark Queen soon.

"Even in my dream, she said 'the more we hide, she'll keep attacking.' I know it sounds like I'm rushing things, but I feel like we need to take action."

Silence fell as the elements exchanged looks before Sun-he spoke again.

"If we're going to fight the Dark Queen, we need to be prepared," she said, smiling at Angelina.

"It's gonna be hard, but I think we can do it," Suez agreed. The other elements gave Angelina an agreeing smile.

"Alright, then it's settled," Angelina declared.
For days the elements of creation trained, perfecting their powers and fighting, all while growing stronger.

They planned out the battle, making sure there wasn't a fatal mistake in it. Eventually, they were ready. Soon the night before the war arrived, and the elements went to bed early to be rested for the important day ahead of them.

Yet Angelina couldn't sleep with her mind spinning with thoughts and fear.

How are we going to defeat the Dark Queen? What will happen if we don't win? She knew the consequences if they didn't win.

The Dark Queen would rule the land again, leaving it to remain in the same dark, grim hell that she had left it for years.

Except this time, no one would have the hope or faith they had for their princess to return and free them. They would have to accept their fate and suffer through the pain once again. And what would happen to her friends back on Earth?

They'd still be searching for Angelina. After that, they'd come to the reality that she was most likely dead, not even having a chance to say good-bye.

Angelina could feel her stomachache as she got deeper into those thoughts. She closed her eyes, shutting down and going to sleep.

CHAPTER SEVENTEEN
BATTLE FOR THE THRONE

THE NIGHT BEFORE THE BATTLE seemed to last forever, but when morning rose, it felt it had come too quick. The girls met up at breakfast. They ate lightly, not wanting overeating to get in the way, but enough to give them energy. Afterward, they trained for one last moment before coming together. Bravery, fear, and determination swirled in their stomachs.

"I can't believe this is happening," Opal said.

"I know, I can't either," said Suez.

"Before we go, there's something I wanted to give you all," Ellie announced. Everyone turned their attention to her. Ellie pulled out six bracelets, each designed to match each person's element.

"I made these at the sleepover. I wanted to make something so that we can have something with us. If we ever get separated or lost, just look at the bracelet, and we'll still be together."

"These are beautiful, Ellie," complimented Sun-he.

"They are," agreed Opal.

"Thank you, Ellie. I'll make sure to wear it all the time," April said.

"I'm not a jewelry person, but this is an exception," Suez said, smiling at Ellie.

"I also wanted to say something," Angelina began. "Look, I know this seems impossible. We all feel scared and even a little doubtful. But we can do this. It may seem impossible, but we just need to have faith in ourselves and watch each other's backs. This kingdom has suffered at the hands of the Dark Queen for far too long. We can't let her destroy it any more than she has."

Hope and bravery sparked in the element's eyes as they listened to Angelina, her words shattering all fear they once felt.

"After all, we are the elements of creation, the protectors of this kingdom. It's our duty to fight all evil and bring in the light." Together the elements of creation raised their hands in a mighty fist.

"Magictopia!" they chanted. "Alright, let's go," Angelina announced.

The elements of creation marched to the Dark Queen's castle, their heads high, ready to take her down once and for all.

What they didn't know was that the Dark Queen was watching them through her specter's crystal ball.

***

"IT'S TIME," she said. The Dark Queen left the throne room with her wand in hand. She entered a vast place, one that looked used for training and battles.

A massive army of soldiers in battle armor in perfect formation was in the chamber. They had a grim, blank expression on their faces and had cold, stiff eyes that were immune to emotion.

They kneeled before her when she stood in front of them.

"Rise," the Dark Queen demanded. They stood to their feet, waiting to hear what she was saying next.

"As you all may know, we're fighting against the elements of creation. But I want today to go down as the day we kill the lost princess and the elements of creation for good! Letting not a single strand of hope or light to ever come into the hearts of the people ever again! Today is the day all light dies, and darkness rules!"

The monsters roared with cheer, chanting, "Let darkness rise!" The Dark Queen's full lips curved into a wicked smile.

"Let the battle begin."

***

THE ELEMENTS OF CREATION reached the Dark Queen's castle. The wind blew a bitter and cold breeze, filling the girls with fear and optimism.

"This is it," said Angelina. "There's no turning back now." A massive cloud of dark magic appeared. It began spinning, forming into a giant illusion of the Dark Queen.

"Looks like you finally came. After all, I'd thought you were too scared to come, but it appears I was wrong."

"You're the one who's too scared to fight! You can't even fight us face to face!" objected Angelina. "And once we defeat you, Magictopia will no longer suffer under your rule!"

The Dark Queen let out a grim chuckle.

"Such brave words for someone who's not even brave themselves. In that case, let the war begin."

She disappeared into the air. The elements kept alert, waiting for the first attack. To their surprise, nothing happened. The faint sound of yelling boomed from far away. The elements froze, wondering what it was. The sound grew louder.

The girls stood in shock when they saw an army of monsters charging at them.

"They're coming!" said April.

"Alright, Suez, you and Sun-he get that side, April and Opal, you get the left. Ellie and I will get the middle, just like we planned," ordered Angelina.

The elements nodded in agreement, positioning themselves in a ready stance.

"Finally, I've been waiting for this moment!" exclaimed Suez, her eyes lighting up with excitement. Together, they charged at the army.

Ellie shot an arrow at a monster, and she did the same with another. A crowd stormed at her; she gathered her energy and shot the most potent arrow.

The arrow blasted the monsters back. Opal smacked every monster she saw with her whip. A wave of them charged at her, and Opal slapped the monsters away with her whip.

Suddenly dozens of monsters charged at her. She turned, and more came from the right. She looked at her whip and smiled. She caught a monster and spun him around and around as fast as she could, hitting all the monsters. The monsters flew all over the place, crashing to the ground.

April smacked every monster she saw as if they were annoying flies. A giant monster came charging at her. April spotted him, and with all her might, she whacked the creature out of sight.

Sun-he blasted her ice at the monsters, and they froze like statues. She clashed her halberd against another monster's sword. The beast pushed her to the ground and waved his sword at her.

Sun-he used all her strength to push him off. She kicked his legs and, with a neat swift of her weapon, slashed the monster out of sight.

***

MEANWHILE, Suez was having a blast. She was knocking out monsters from left to right.

"Take that!" she said as she kicked a monster in the face. A monster picked her up from behind and tossed her to the ground.

Suez was dizzy for a moment, then regained her strength and got back on her feet.

"Oh, you asked for it!" she growled. Her fists were on fire, and so were her eyes. She could set someone on fire if she just looked at them. She punched the monster so hard, he caught on fire, and he screamed in pain.

"That's right! No one messes with the element of fire!" said Suez, putting her hands on her hips. Angelina blasted golden beams at the monsters; a monster ran towards her. She tossed her shield and hit the monster's head, and he fell. Another shot an arrow, she blocked it, and the shaft bounced back and shot him.

A beast tried to sneak behind her. Angelina heard him coming. She jumped up high, flipped in the air, and blasted a beam, and tossed her shield at the monster. She landed on the ground; the rest of the elements ran to her.

"Finally, that part's over," sighed Angelina. "Now, we get to the Dark Queen."

The Dark Queen's illusion reappeared, and the elements watched in a ready stance waiting for what would happen next.

"Looks like you've cleared the first army. I must admit I'm quite impressed. But let's see how you do with the next one." She disappeared once again.

"Looks like we have more work on our hands before we can get to her," Sun-he said.

"Aw, man! We just finished the last one. How much bigger is the next one!?" said Suez. Just as she finished her sentence, the elements turned to see another army of monsters twice as gigantic, tougher, and powerful than the last that came out.

"Um, twice as big," answered April.

"C'mon girls, we can't give up!" said Angelina.

"We do the same as last time, got it?" The elements nodded in agreement. With that, they charged at the monsters. But this army was no doubt more powerful than the last.

They shot fire arrows at the girls; the elements were too late to block them, and they were hit by the arrows. Ellie took to the air, shooting arrows at the army; the monsters did the same. Ellie fluttered past the hits, yet she wasn't fast enough.

Two darts sliced broad cuts in her arm, making her bleed. Ellie winced in pain as she tried regaining herself and fired back at the monsters.

Opal cracked her whip at an elf. The elf grabbed the whip and slapped Opal across her face. The elf kept hitting her before she could react. Bruises slowly formed on Opal's face. She pulled out another whip, smacking the elf back.

While he was down, Opal wrapped her weapon around him, using all her strength and might to spin him around and around. Opal waited until he was high enough in the air to let him go, launching him across the land.

April was fighting a pixie; she pointed her staff at him, shooting massive long vines darted at him as he charged at her. But the pixie cut through vines.

April tried to block them off again, but the pixie kicked her across the ground before she could do anything, scraping her arm.

Before she could get up, he struck her again. April raised her hand, and thorned vines emerged from the ground and grabbed the pixie.

April put him in the air, then crashed him back down. Sun-he blasted ice beams and cold winter winds at groups of magical beings.

The creatures shot fire bolts at her. Sun-he was too busy fighting to see the bolts coming her way and hit her, leaving her shoulder and arm burned. Sun-he turned back to the creatures, finishing them off by freezing them with her magic.

Suez was surrounded by monsters.

"Bring it," dared Suez in a bold, brave tone. The monsters attacked her all at once, Suez's fist lit on fire, and she punched and blasted fireballs at them.

"Yeah, take that, punks!" she said. Suez was on a roll knocking them out. But she wasn't as successful when a monster caught her punch in his hand. Suez used her free hand to strike him again, but the demon grabbed her hand and punched her face.

He finished his attack by tossing her across the field.

"Man, these guys are tough!" said Suez. She slowly got up, holding her stomach. She wiped the blood dripping from her nose. Suez ran up to the monster, finishing him off with a flaming punch.

Angelina fought against a monster with a sharp sword. The fiend clashed his sword on her shield. Angelina pushed the beast back and shot a powerful beam at him; the beast dodged her attack.

He grabbed her by the shield and forced her to the ground. The monster clashed down his sword once again and began moving down against Angelina's cover.

Angelina used all her strength to shove back the beast, all while nearly being crushed. She shot a beam of light at the beast, blasting the monster off her.

As the battle continued, more and more demons came, making the girls tired and weak. They put all of their energy into every kick, punch, hit, and blast.

But they still weren't fast or strong enough to block off the monster's attacks, leaving them with bruises and injuries.

Soon they were able to defeat almost all of the army. Only a few of the monsters remained. The girls fell to the ground in exhaustion, trying to gather up more energy to fight.

A small group of monsters charged at them. Angelina stood up, and with the last bit of her strength, she hit them with a massive blast of light, defeating the monsters once and for all. Angelina fell back to the ground.

"That's the last of them." she sighed.

"Did you think that was it?" boomed the Dark Queen's sinister voice, along with her illusion.

The girls stood quick on their feet.

"You've defeated all the armies, but there's one last thing you still have to finish." Her illusion disappeared, and there standing with a wicked smile were the elements of destruction. The girls gasped when they saw them.

"We have to defeat them?"

"Isn't this a treat? We get to kill the elements of creation a second time. Only this time will be even more enjoyable to finish," Rebecca remarked.

"I wouldn't be so cocky if I were you. We're stronger than you could possibly think!" fired back Opal. As the girls got in their battle stance, Ellie put her hand on Angelina's shoulder. Angelina turned to her with a puzzled look.

"Go," said Ellie.

"What?" asked Angelina.

"Go," said Ellie. "We'll deal with these guys, go fight the queen."

"I can't just leave you guys here!" said Angelina.

"Go on, kid, we can handle them. Besides, you have a throne to claim!" assured Suez. Angelina couldn't believe what she was hearing. She looked at her friends, who gave her a reassuring smile.

"Go, we got this," said Ellie, with a confident smile.

Relieved, Angelina smiled back at them and ran off to find the Dark Queen. A golden speck of light from her necklace led towards a huge, dark temple.

When Angelina reached the temple's front, the wind blew through her hair, giving her a weird and bold feeling.

She took a deep breath and walked in. Inside no one was there.

"Hey, I know you're in here!" yelled Angelina. "You're saying that I'm hiding, but you're the one hiding. Maybe you're the scared one." An eerie silence fell, sending chills down Angelina's spine.

"So, we meet again," said a cold voice. Angelina turned around to where the voice had come from. In its place, a cloud of darkness formed and the Dark Queen emerged. She gave Angelina her classic evil smile.

"I'm surprised you've made it this far. I'd thought by now you would be gone."

"That's enough!" Angelina demanded. "You've ruled this world long enough! You've destroyed all the light and good in this world, putting fear into people's hearts. But, now, your reign will end!"

Angelina's dark brown eyes gave her a fierce stare. The Dark Queen laughed to herself.

"You know, you remind me so much of your mother." Her lips curved into a twisted smile.

Angelina's eyes filled up with tears, anger filling her heart. She blasted a golden beam at the Dark Queen, and the queen caught it in her hands. She turned the beam black, shooting it back at Angelina.

Angelina put up her shield, but the hit pushed her hard to the floor. Angelina got up and charged at the queen.

The Dark Queen brought out her specter, blasting dark beams at Angelina. Angelina moved left and right, missing them. She stroked her shield.

The Dark Queen pushed back with her scepter. She began pushing down Angelina with her strength. Angelina struggled to get against her. As she was slowly being forced to the floor, The Dark Queen aimed her hand at her, blasting her across the room and slamming into the wall. Bruises began to form on Angelina's skin as she got up to fight again.

**

THE REST OF THE ELEMENTS were up against a giant, dark elemental monster and the elements of destruction. The beast let out a massive roar while fire and ice stones shot out of its mouth.

April and Suez fended off the rocks while the others went after the dark elements.

"Soon, you brats will be nothing but dead meat!" said Rick.

The dark elements added to the monster's attacks with theirs. Ellie fired a dozen arrows at the beast, and the arrows sank in the creature's stomach.

The monster fired back the arrows out of its hand. This time they were bigger and on fire. The girls jumped past the arrows, Suez took a step forward toward the monster.

"Alright ya, big rock lump, it's time you see what the 'Sizzling Suez' can do!" said Suez. She ran at the monster, her fist lighting up, and gave it a huge fire punch in the stomach.

The beast tumbled a little, molded a dark root ball, and rolled it at the elements. They all moved out of the way.

"Maybe the 'Sizzling Suez' should sizzle it down!" growled an annoyed Sun-he.

"I wonder how Angelina's doing," said Ellie.

***

BUT ANGELINA WAS DOING WORSE; her training was nothing compared to the queen.

Angelina tossed her shield along with a vast beam of light. The Dark Queen blasted a ball of dark magic, destroying Angelina's attack. The ball came flying towards Angelina. Angelina jumped before it could hit her, pulling out another shield and charging at the Dark Queen.

The Dark Queen grabbed her arm, punching Angelina in the stomach before throwing her to the ground. More bruises were left on Angelina, along with a heavy flow of blood from her nose.

Angelina laid on their floor, trying to regain enough strength, yet she could barely get up.

The Dark Queen walked towards her and grabbed her by her neck.

Angelina struggled to free herself.

"You know, I never thought I would get to fight you," the Dark Queen began to speak.

"I thought years ago that I had killed all of the royal family. After all, I did it with my own hands." She smiled as Angelina gritted her teeth in anger.

"But, I'm glad you came because now I have the chance to end you for sure this time."

The Dark Queen tossed her across the temple once again; Angelina laid there, too hurt to stand.

She hoped that the rest of the elements were doing better than her.

***

BUT THE ELEMENTS WERE STRUGGLING as well, with the elements of destruction and the monster having the upper hand.

"I think it's time we finish the elements of creation once and for all!" Gage announced.

Together the dark elements and the monster used their magic to create a huge dark rainbow.

The elements of creation pushed back with their weapons. Slowly they were being overthrown by the dark elements. The girls used all their might to save themselves from their dark fate.

"You know it's almost sad," Rebecca began.

"Magictopia's last hope, the elements of creation are about to disappoint like the last. It just shows what a pathetic display you all are. You come to avenge the kingdom only to fail. At least you won't be here much longer."

The elements of destruction increased their magic; at this point, they were crushing the elements of creation.

The girls didn't give up, draining all their power into fighting back. They couldn't give up; they just couldn't.

They all had come so far, together—working side by side, living under the Dark Queen's rule, having suffered all those years. And then there was Angelina.

They couldn't let her down either; she had brought them together, given them hope when they didn't have it.

They couldn't give up, not now. They had to live for the kingdom, Angelina, and themselves.

Together the elements of creation used all of their energy to make their own powerful rainbow of power.

The blast was enough to destroy the monster and the elements of destruction once and for all. Smoke filled the air, slightly covering everything. The elements collapsed in exhaustion once they knew they won.

"Finally, it's over!" sighed Sun-he, exhausted.

"Really? Oh, don't I think so!" said a voice in the smoke.

The girls jumped to their feet, looking for who spoke. As the smoke cleared up, the elements froze in shock when they saw...Angela.

"*WAIT!* How are you still here!?" said a stunned Opal.

"No matter how hard you try, you can never get rid of me!" remarked Angela. She shot a huge, dark beam. The elements jumped up, dodging her hit.

Angela shot again, this time hitting them. Ellie shot a few arrows at Angela. Angela used her magic to stop the arrows and dart them back at Ellie.

Ellie wasn't quick enough to dodge, and they grazed her arms, making them bleed.

Opal cracked her whip at Angela and kicked it. She formed a water tentacle and darted it.

Angela destroyed it with a blast of dark energy and blasted more dark magic at Opal, pushing her to the ground.

Sun-he charged at her and flashed her halberd. Angela dodged it and kicked her. Sun-he got up and threw ice shards at Angela. Angela dodged the shards and created dark orbs, charging them at Sun-he.

Sun-he was able to miss the first orbs, but she was hit with the last few, causing Sun-he to be tossed across the battlefield.

"That's it! Nobody messes with my friends!" said April. She raised her hand high. Thick vines grew from the ground and soared into the air.

The roots came at Angela, but Angela's hand glowed with magic, turning them black and gaining control.

With a wave of her hand, the vines came hurtling back at April, throwing her high in the air. April crashed to the ground.

Sun-he gathered the elements and whispered to them.

"Guys, I have an idea. April and I will hold Angela down. The rest of you hit her with your best attacks."

"Sounds good," agreed Suez.

"I hope this works," said April.

Sun-he and April charged at Angela, April grew roots from the ground and wrapped them tightly around Angela's wrists and ankles, Sun-he froze her whole body with frost and ice.

They watched as Angela struggled to free herself; Sun-he smiled at the fact her plan was working.

They watched as Ellie, Opal, and Suez jumped high and blasted their attacks at Angela.

But just as the plan was about to work, Angela used her dark magic to free herself and kill off the element's attack on her.

Angela then turned to the elements and blasted them with a ball of magic, knocking them to the ground. When the girls tried to get up, they were shocked to find themselves frozen, with a dark light around them.

"Hey! What's happening!?" said Ellie, struggling to move. Angela walked up to them with a grim look on her face.

"You better let us go!" demanded Suez. If she wasn't frozen, she would've punched Angela by now.

"I don't think so. By the time I get to you, you'll already be dead," said Angela grimly.

"Maybe then you'll think twice before you even think of trying to steal our kingdom."

"*WHAT!?* We're not the ones trying to take the kingdom! It's the Dark Queen!" objected Opal.

"She's the one who stole Magictopia and killed the true rulers," Ellie added.

"Do you honestly expect me to believe such lies?" demanded Angela. "I already know what you're doing. Mother told me all about how you've been trying to steal the throne for yourselves!"

"We're not trying to steal anything. It's your mom who killed the king and queen and lied to you," said Suez.

"Enough!" Angela objected. "I've heard plenty of your lies, and they won't save you now. Get ready for your death." She raised one hand at the elements. Magic formed. It glowed brighter, ready to shoot.

Suddenly, the elements' jewelry glowed. Light emerged from them, shaping into an illusion of fourteen years ago.

There it showed the same woman from Angelina's dream, her long black curls floating in the air and her blue eyes glistening. She stood inside the castle, holding a baby wrapped in a blanket. The woman smiled sweetly at her child.

"Angela, I know you're only a couple months old, so you won't remember me..." the woman stopped as tears filled her eyes, and she choked with emotion.

She was making the difficult decision of having to give up her child, having to miss her to grow into a woman, not being there to witness her accomplishments.

She didn't want to, but she had no choice—the woman composed herself before she continued talking.

"But I want you to know...how much I love you...and I'm only doing this to protect you."

She wiped her tears and smiled at her baby once more. The woman gave the child a necklace that looked like Angelina's, but it was a darker gold shade. The woman kneeled down and gently put her baby in a basket.

"Well, well, well," boomed a cold voice. The woman turned in fear when she saw the Dark Queen standing steps away from her.

"Alexis!" "Amanda," said the Dark Queen, with an evil grin.

"I thought you might be here, trying to save your poor child from the same fate her father faced." The baby began to cry. Amanda held her close.

"Even she knows her fate is sealed," the Dark Queen said grimly.

"Alexis, you don't have to do this," Amanda began as she stood up. "I know deep inside there's still the same sweet, smart, strong young lady I know. And I'm not saying that for my sake. I'm saying it for yours."

The Dark Queen didn't say anything, only responding with a dull expression, until she roared with sick laughter.

"Oh, Amanda, you're always so compassionate. Always seeing the good in people, believing that they could change."

The Dark Queen pulled out her dark scepter.

"But, you failed to notice that not everyone is good inside." She blasted her scepter at Amanda.

There was nothing left but her screams, smoke, and a crying baby. The Dark Queen walked over to the baby and picked her up.

"Perhaps, something could become useful out of you," she said as she touched the baby's cheek.

"*Shh, shh*, everything's okay, *mommy's here*."

The vision disappeared. Angela stood there, taking in the new information she had just witnessed as she wiped her tears. She fell to the ground, her world shattered.

Everything she was told was a lie. A cold, dirty lie. The woman she had thought to be her mother had murdered her real mother. She had destroyed everything she didn't know she had, corrupted her, and made her into one of her creations of destruction.

The Dark Queen had taken everything from her. Angela's mind then wandered to Angelina.

Angelina...her sister, was no doubt in trouble.

That was if the Dark Queen hadn't finished her yet.

"I have to stop her!" Angela declared, standing to her feet. Before she left, she turned to the elements of creation, freeing them from her magic.

"Thank you and hurry. There's no telling how Angelina's doing," said Ellie.

"Right," Angela nodded. She stopped and turned back to them once more.

"Thank you." Angela took off flying into the air, heading towards the temple Angelina and the Dark Queen were located. When Angela reached the temple, she found Angelina lying on the ground hurt, and the Dark Queen getting ready to finish her off for good.

"*STOP!*" shouted Angela. The Dark Queen turned, flabbergasted to see Angela.

"Angela!" she gasped. She quickly composed herself. Her fake loving smile curved on her lips, and her voice changed to a motherly tone.

"Actually, I'm glad you're here," she began. She pushed her scepter into Angelina's back while she faced Angela.

"Do you want to join your mother in killing this thief once and for all?" Angela looked at Angelina's face, her eyes filled with fear and tears. Bruises, cuts, and blood covered her battered body; she gazed at Angela with almost pleading eyes.

"You liar! You've lied to me my whole life!" shouted Angela.

"Honey, what are you talking about?" asked the Queen.

"You killed my parents, brainwashed me, and now you're trying to make me kill my sister! You took everything from me, turned me into one of your weapons!" The Dark Queen's sweet smile was replaced with a cruel grin, and she let out a grim laugh.

"So, after all these years, you've figured it out," she said.

"At first, I didn't want to raise you, but I figured I could grow you into a weapon—something I could use. But now I see. You're capable of much, much more. We can both rule the kingdom together!" The Dark Queen offered her hand out to Angela.

"What do you say, sweetie?" she said in her fake loving voice. Angela looked at Angelina's beaten and bruised body. She thought about the pain she caused her and her family. All the lies Angela was told. All caused by the Dark Queen.

"*NEVER!* You lied to me my whole life, and I won't make the same mistake as you did fourteen years ago!" The Dark Queen dropped her hand.

"Well, if that's what you really want."

Angela blasted dark beams at the queen.

The Dark Queen dodged the beams. She swayed her arm towards Angela, and a wave of dark beams charged at her.

Angela flew around, trying to avoid the beams, but she wasn't fast enough. The rays hit her, and she crashed to the ground. Angela slowly got up and stomped her foot.

A massive wave of dark power headed for the Dark Queen; she stood still, just as the tide was about to crash into her. Then it turned to crystal and shattered into pieces.

The Dark Queen raised her hand; her magic took control of Angela, tossing her into the air.

She tossed Angela violently against the walls and ceiling like a doll. She threw her in the air once more, this time striking Angela with a bolt of darkness. Angela fell to the floor next to Angelina. She was just as bruised as her. Angela tried to rise back up, reaching a hand out to move. But she was already drained and beaten, no energy left to move. The Dark Queen took a step up to the twins, a satisfied grin on her face.

"Now this is a sight. I killed the old rulers of this land once long ago. I watched as I slaughtered them with my bare hands, watching their blood pour. This time I get the chance to do it again, only this time will be even better!" She grabbed her scepter, pointing it at the twins. Darkness charged at her scepter tip, ready to hit. Angelina looked up, collecting her bit of power to lift her hand in an attempt to form a shield. A golden spark flashed but quickly faded away.

"*HA!* Do you honestly think you can stop me? You're powerless!" The Dark Queen mocked.
She shot with all her power...all there was left was black smoke, covering everything, a malicious smile curved on the Dark Queen's full lips.

But her smile faded when she saw a golden light shining through the smoke.

The Dark Queen's eyes widened with shock and disbelief. To her horror, Angelina had put up a golden shield!

"*WHAT!?*" screamed the Dark Queen.

"*HOW IS THAT POSSIBLE!?*" She blasted the twins again, Angelina's shield blocked off the hit once more. The Dark Queen tried again, again, and again, but each hit was blocked off. She aimed her hand at Angela and fired at her. A dark golden sword appeared in Angela's hand and blocked the shot.

"*WHAT!?*" The Dark Queen objected.

She couldn't believe her eyes when she saw the twins were lifted into the air by golden light. The light circled them, making their hair grow long.

Angelina now wore a beautiful, long, golden dress made of lace, with golden knee-high boots and gloves. Angela wore a long, off-the-shoulder dark golden dress, a diamond-encrusted belt around her. The dress came with matching knee-high boots and gloves. A dark golden locket that looked the same as Angelina's also flashed on her neck.

They both wore a golden tiara filled with gems. A golden shield with diamonds and steel angel wings appeared in Angelina's hand. A dark golden sword with diamonds in it and steel angel wings came into Angela's hand. Together the twins raised their hands and formed a giant ball of light.

The Dark Queen slowly backed away as the light blinded her. The twins brought down their hands, and the ball of light came crashing down at the Dark Queen.

"NO, I'M THE RIGHTFUL QUEEN! NOOOOOOOO!" cried the queen.

The light dissolved her, leaving nothing else but a dark light that vanished with her. The twins turned face-to-face and held hands. A golden light emerged from them to all of Magictopia. Everyone in the kingdom watched, bursting with joy, knowing that they were now free.

"They did it!" cheered the elements of creation. They hugged each other while letting out laughs of happiness and relief. Once they finished celebrating, they hurried to the temple to see Angelina and Angela lying on the floor. The twins slowly woke when the elements came and embraced them.

"We did it!" April announced.

"Finally, the Dark Queen is gone!" Sun-he joined in.

"And the kingdom is free. We don't have to live in fear anymore!" Suez chimed. Their celebration was cut short when they heard Angela sobbing.

"I'm...sorry, I didn't know. I… hurt you all… I betrayed my own kingdom," she said through her tears. Angelina wrapped her arms around her sister and gave her a tight hug.

"It's okay, you didn't know," she assured.

"I know, but I still caused all that pain to you all," sobbed Angela. Ellie put her hand on Angela's shoulder.

"You don't have to be so hard on yourself. You were a victim of the Dark Queen too. She lied and manipulated you. It's not your fault."

"Yeah, and we forgive you for almost killing us," said Sun-he, half-joking and half genuine.

"Well, I'm not ready to forgive just yet," Suez teased, smiling at Angela. They laughed and walked over to the temple window. Magictopia was finally free. It was almost hard to believe.

"We did it," said April softly.

"Yeah, all of the fighting is gone," agreed Angelina.

"Looks like our work here is done," said Ellie.

"There's only one thing I need to do now," said Angelina. Everyone turned to her, wondering what she meant. "I need to go back to Earth. And tell all my friends I'm safe. There's no doubt they've been worried."

The others nodded.

Together they used their jewelry to create a rainbow portal back to Earth and transported through it.

CHAPTER EIGHTEEN
HOME

THEY MADE IT HOME in front of Miss A's orphanage. Angelina walked up to the front door. She tried knocking on the door, but she stopped.

Come on, Angelina, you can do this, she told herself. She knocked on the door. Ms. A opened the door and froze as she saw Angelina.

"Angel...Angelina?" she said, tears running down her cheeks. "It's really you." Angelina nodded, and Ms. A hugged her as if she were her own. "Thank God you're alive! I was scared to death," said Ms. A.

"I know, I'm sorry." apologized Angelina. When Ms. A let her go, her eyes were locked on Angelina's enormous angel wings.

"Um… Angelina..." she stuttered. Angelina gave her a nervous smile and began to explain.

"Actually, Ms. A... While I was gone, I found out that I'm a half-angel princess and part of a magical group called the elements of creation, which protects a magical land called Magictopia, which I just freed from my crazy, evil aunt."

Ms. A gave a confused and strange look; she looked back at the elements who waved awkwardly at her, then looked back at Angelina.

Ms. A stood there for a moment, processing the news. Her face twisted then with shock and confusion.

"I-I can't believe it… you… the necklace..."

"I know it was hard for me even to believe it myself." Angelina began. "But I'm still the same girl you've known and love. I just happen to have some magic ancestry." Ms. A looked up at her, taking deep breaths.

"Well...I'm just glad you're safe..." Ms. A said, trying to form a smile

"And while I was gone, I found out I have a twin," said Angelina. She motioned to Angela. Angela slowly walked up next to her and smiled shyly. Ms. A looked at both of them and smiled.

"You're beautiful, just like your sister," she said. "I have some people who would love to meet you."

She brought the girls inside the house.

"Hey, girls, Angelina's back!" announced Ms. A. The girls came running down the stairs and gasped with excitement when they saw Angelina.

"Angelina!" they exclaimed. They all crowded around her and hugged her. Leona, Avery, and Sophia came up towards Angelina.

"Guys! It's so great to see you!" Angelina beamed with happiness.

"Angelina! We're so glad you're safe," said Sophia, relieved.

"Angelina, we came to apologize," said Leona.

"The day you ran off, we figured it was our fault for not running after you."

"You're our sister, and we should've helped you at that time. We were worried that you were dead, thanks to us," Avery added.

"We're sorry," said Sophia.

"Guys, it's not your fault what happened to me," assured Angelina. "Besides, I found out that I'm a princess of a magical land and have a twin sister." Her friends glanced at her with disbelief.

Angelina raised her wings, and they shimmered in the light. Everyone gazed at them in astonishment, taking in the fantastic sight of Angelina's massive wings. Silence filled the room for a few minutes, and the atmosphere became awkward until eyes widened in realization and shock.

"*OH MY GOD*! It is true!" yelled Sophia.

"I... I can't believe it..." gasped Leona.

"Wait, did you just say you have a twin too!?" exclaimed Avery. Angela came into the scene.

"Guys, this is my twin sister, Angela," said Angelina. Angela smiled shyly and blushed.

"Hello," she greeted.

"Oh my god! She's amazing!" Leona gasped excitedly.

"And I also made some friends from Magicopia," said Angelina. She turned around to find the elements surrounded by a crowd of all the foster girls.

They all talked at once, asking them all about Magictopia. "Looks like everyone else has met them," said Angelina.

They joined in the crowd. Angelina settled all the girls down in a circle. They passed the time by telling everyone what happened on their journey and answered any questions that were given.

"Angelina," called Ms. A.

Angelina walked up to her.

"Is everything okay, Ms. A?" Angelina asked.

"I need to talk to you about something," Ms. A replied in a serious tone. Angelina nodded, worry showing on her face. They parted from everyone else, and Ms. A spoke.

"Angelina, days after I called the police when you went missing, a woman called me. She claimed that she was your aunt. I told the police about it, yet they didn't look into it too much. I feel in my heart that she truly is, or she wouldn't bother looking for you. But I thought it was worth mentioning that she might be your aunt."

Angelina looked at her with wide eyes filling up with tears.

"Re... really?" she asked, her voice cracking with emotion. Ms. A handed her a piece of paper with an address on it.

"She gave me her address in case you ever came back." Angelina looked at the paper, then looked up at Ms. A.

"Thank you... Ms. A" Ms. A smiled at her.

"You're welcome."

Angelina walked up to the elements of creation.

"Guys, we have one more mission to complete."

Ms. A, the elements of creation, and a few girls from the orphanage hopped in the car and drove to the written address. The trip was longer than they had expected; two whole hours seemed to be forever.

"Are you nervous?" asked Angela.

"More than anything. I'm finally about to meet my aunt after all these years, who isn't a psycho," said Angelina. "And all those years of wondering about my real family, what they were like. I'm just kinda nervous if she'll like me or if she's a good person."

"Well, don't worry. Because this time, I'm right by your side," said Angela. She held her sister's hand, squeezing it as a sign of support and reassurance. Angelina smiled back at her. It felt so crazy to have a twin sister all this time; she had always wondered if she had any siblings she didn't know about. Though she wished they met differently, maybe where they weren't enemies. But in the end, she had a sister, and she couldn't be any happier.

They finally parked in front of a white house and got out of the car. Angelina and Angela walked up to the door. Their bodies trembled with fear and uncertainty; their worlds were changing so fast they didn't know what to do. The twins embraced hands and faced each other.

"You ready?" asked Angelina.

"Yeah," said Angela. They both took a deep breath, and Angela knocked on the door. A woman opened it. The woman looked to be in her late thirties to early forties. She was a petite woman with short black hair and bangs over her dark brown eyes. Her skin was a mocha tone. She wore a dark blue shirt with the sleeves rolled up, gray pants, and sneakers.

"Hello, can I help you?" the woman asked.

"Yes, are you Jerrica Golden?" asked Angelina.

"Yes," said the woman.

"We heard that fourteen years ago, your younger brother and sister-in-law died along with their twin daughters," said Angela. The woman's eyes dropped with sadness when she heard Angela.

"Sadly, yes," she replied softly.

"We.... want you to know that your twin nieces are still alive. And we know where they are," said Angela. The woman's eyes opened wide with hope.

"Really!? Where are they?" she asked anxiously.

"Actually…" said Angelina." The twins took a step forward. "We're your nieces." Jerrica stared at them in confusion.

"Wait," she said. She scrutinized the two girls, a beaming smile coming on her, and her eyes filled with tears of joy.

"Real… real… Really?" The twins nodded and hugged their aunt.

"Oh, I thought I lost you all," she sobbed.

"But, wait, I thought Magictopia was taken over," said Aunt Jerrica.

"Don't worry; we freed it. With our friends here," said Angelina. Jerrica looked up at the elements of creation, they waved, and she waved back.

"Well, it looks like I have two angel nieces," said Jerrica. She hugged her nieces again, and everyone clapped and smiled.

CHAPTER NINETEEN
A NEW AGE

TWO MONTHS HAD PASSED by. Magictopia had gotten its original color and light back with the great rule of its crown princesses and the elements of creation. The crowning ceremony of the twins was set up with the entire kingdom of Magictopia, as well as many friends and family of the twins. Aunt Jerrica had adopted the twins and was brought to Magictopia by creating a portal with the other elements' help. Angelina would stay in Magictopia to rule over the land with the elements of creation, but she would still visit Earth as much as possible to keep in touch with Ms. A and her friends from the orphanage.

Eventually, Angelina told Max everything that had happened. Of course, it took him, Ms. A, and the girls from the orphanage a while to understand everything thoroughly, but they were able to accept it over time.

"Citizens of Magictopia, thank you all for coming. As you know, fourteen years ago, my brother and his wife were killed by the Dark Queen's evil, but my two nieces were still alive, and they found a way to stop her," announced Aunt Jerrica.

"Because of their bravery, they will be rightfully crowned as Magictopia's crown princesses. Jerrica picked up a golden tiara filled with all sorts of sparkling gems, with tiny, golden angel wings on each side. Aunt Jerrica carefully placed the sparkling tiara on Angelina's head and kissed her forehead.

"This is so beautiful," said Ellie, wiping her tears of joy. "Just look how happy they are. I'm just so happy."

"Ease it with the tears, Ellie. You're gonna make me soft if you keep doing that," teased Suez, lightly punching Ellie's arm. Jerrica grabbed a dark golden tiara that looked just like Angelina's. The only difference was that the gems were placed differently. She put it on Angela as she kissed her cheek.

"Ladies and gentlemen, your princesses of Magictopia," said Aunt Jerrica.

The crowd cheered and clapped as loud as they could. "And now may the elements of creation come up, please?" asked Aunt Jerrica.

The elements hurried to the stage, wondering what Jerrica had planned. "My nieces couldn't have defeated the Dark Queen without these young girls, and so please give the elements of creation a hand!" The crowd applauded loud and proud for their princesses and elements of creation. The elements smiled proudly. They had done it. It was almost like a dream, except it was real.

"We did it, girls!" Angelina said, beaming with joy.

"Yeah, and we did it together," said Sun-he.

"Hey, is this a party or what!?" said Opal. The girls got off the stage and headed to the dance floor, leaving Angelina and Angela alone.

"Hey," said Angelina.

"Hey," replied Angela. There was a short silence between the two sisters.

"Thank you," said Angela.

"For what?" asked Angelina.

"For giving me a second chance,"

"Of course. You're my sister; besides, you didn't mean any harm,"

"Yes, but..." Angelina hugged her sister tightly.

"Angela, it's okay. That's all in the past now. Besides, we need to move on for the future."

Angela smiled.

"You're right. Besides, I have you to help me through it."

"Excuse me, may I have this dance?" A young lady asked Angela. Angela turned to Angelina for advice.

"Go on," said Angelina. Angela followed the young lady to the dance floor. Angelina smiled as she watched her sister dance.

"Excuse me, madam, may I have this dance?" asked a familiar voice. Angelina turned around to see Max with a smile on his face.

"Why you may, sir," she said, tagging along. She grabbed his hand, and the two headed to the dance floor and showed off their dance moves with all their friends. The whole day, the elements of creation danced and laughed with their friends and family. Angelina and Angela met some of their relatives, and some Magictopians came by to thank them for freeing their land.

The day faded into sunset, and everyone began to leave and thank the elements once more. Angelina stood in front of a massive window in the castle, gazing at the golden and rose sunset.

"What a beautiful view," said Max. He walked up to the window and joined her.

"Yeah, the sunset here is amazing," agreed Angelina.

"I can't believe I know someone who's a princess," said Max.

"I know sometimes I can't believe it either," said Angelina. They shared a smile before they flashed red with blush.

"Well, I better get going. You still up for Saturday?" asked Max.

"You bet," said Angelina. Max smiled at her before waving goodbye and leaving. Angelina turned back to the sunset when the elements of creation joined her as well.

"So how does it feel to be the great princess of light?" asked Ellie.

"It's great," said Angelina. "Never in my life have I ever expected anything like this. It's like a dream that I don't ever want to end."

"And the best part is it's real," said Sun-he.

"Do you think we'll be good protectors?" asked Opal. Angelina smiled.

"Trust me, guys, I know it." They all looked upon the golden sunset, knowing that their future was in good hands.

AUTHOR'S NOTE

Looking back now, it's almost crazy to think I've been writing this book for four years. I was eleven, and at the time, this story was just one of many in my head. But I wanted it to be more than just that, and so with the help of my father, I began developing the world. When I first started writing this story, I felt a joy I never really felt before — building the world of Magictopia and the characters that live in it allowed me to put my creativity to use and made working fun. I spent the past years going back and changing the story to make it even better than the last draft. Of course, there were ups and downs during it all. There were times I thought I'd never see the day this thing would be published, and it would just remain a dream in my head. But finally, I'm able to share this story with the world. And just to know that you, the reader took the time to read and invest yourself in this world, and the characters that I love make me so happy. My reason for writing this was to entwine people into a new reality and immerse them in an adventure and maybe even inspire you to pursue your own dreams.

ACKNOWLEDGMENTS

There are so many people I want to shout out and give thanks to. Firstly, my dad; was the one who really kicked this thing off and helped me start writing my first draft. From then on, he continued to encourage, inspire, and give me criticism that really shaped this story into what it is today. He was the one who listened to every little detail or idea I had, saw the passion burning within me, and wanted me to ignite it. You're who I felt so confident and safe with my work, encouraging me to go further. You helped me find my true career and that I was at first unsure. You helped me become a writer, just like you. And for that, I will forever be thankful. I love you.

Of course, I wouldn't have the ability to publish this book without my dear Uncle Antoine, who, in his own way, is like a second father to me. You were the one who heard I wrote a book and gave me the opportunity to spread it out to the world as I had been dying to do for so long. You also were the one who guided me along this journey of starting my career, and you formatted and edited this book—making it even better. I have to admit I was a little scared sharing this story with someone else than dad, mainly because I beat myself up in fear of what people say. But when you told me your genuine love and interest in the story, it sparked confidence in my work. So, thank you, and I love you.

To my mama, thank you for giving me life and for always being the warm sunshine that rids my mind of the dark times where I felt sad. I'm inspired to have the confidence and work ethic that you possess. Thank you for working hard for my sister and me. I know these past years have been hard, especially with us loosing Jazzy. But, I want you to know that all that you've done is very appreciated. You're like my own, Ms. A, the mother who stood with me and loved me no matter what. A chunk of this has been done for you so that you can know your daughter went out and took a step in the world. Thank you so much. I love you.

My grandparents. You have given me your love and support that allowed me to transform this story into much more. Thank you for encouraging and supporting my writing and art. You have given me the tools to pave the way to my journey. I promise you I'm going to do great things in the world.

I want to thank my ninth-grade English teacher, Catherine Lebouton, for reading and giving me feedback that made the story better. Also, for teaching me so I could improve my skills as a writer. Thank you.

And how could I forget you? Yeah, you. The reader. None of this would be possible without you. Thank you so much for reading this story and inviting you into a whole new world. I still have plenty of more stories, characters, and worlds to show you, and I look forward to that.